Her Rogue for Christmas

Her Rogue for Christmas
WICKED WIDOWS' LEAGUE

DAWN BROWER

"...when pain is over, the remembrance of it often becomes a pleasure."

— **JANE AUSTEN, PERSUASION**

Contents

Prologue	1
Chapter 1	9
Chapter 2	18
Chapter 3	28
Chapter 4	39
Chapter 5	49
Chapter 6	60
Chapter 7	71
Chapter 8	82
Epilogue	95
Thank You	99

EXCERPT: HER DUKE TO SAVOR

Prologue	105
Chapter 1	115

EXCERPT: A LADY NEVER TELLS

Blurb	129
Prologue	133
Chapter 1	141
Acknowledgments	157
About Dawn Brower	159
Also by Dawn Brower	161

This is a work of fiction. Names, characters, places, and incidents are products of the author's imagination or are used fictitiously and are not to be construed as real. Any resemblance to actual locales, organizations, or persons, living or dead, is entirely coincidental.

Her Rogue for Christmas © 2024 Dawn Brower

Cover art by Mandy Koehler Designs

All rights reserved. No part of this book may be used or reproduced electronically or in print without written permission, except in the case of brief quotations embodied in reviews.

*For all those that find strength when they need it most.
Do not give up. You never know what you might discover
in the middle of your journey.*

Prologue

Miss Elena Burrows sat beside the fountain in the garden at Haverston House and lifted her face to the sky. The sunlight warmed her skin, spreading over her in waves of delicious heat. It was the day of her birth—the day she would officially be launched into society, finally able to attend balls, soirées, and picnics. She could even go to the theater and the opera. She could hardly wait. At long last, at eight and ten, she would enjoy more freedom—or at least, as much freedom as society's dictates allowed a young lady.

"You look lovely."

Elena started at the sound of a gentleman's voice. Not because she feared it, but because she had not expected it. She had believed herself alone in the garden. Turning, she met his gaze. The man before her was the very one she was most pleased to see. His dark brown hair gleamed in the sunlight, and those pale blue eyes warmed her far more than the sun's rays... The Earl of Northfield was the love of her young life. Elena had adored him for years, and she knew he felt the same.

He held her heart, and she believed his belonged to her. Six years her senior and her brother's closest friend, she had known since the moment they met that she would always love him. He had stolen her heart with his kindness—and it certainly helped that he was perhaps the handsomest man she had ever had the privilege to gaze upon. That meeting was years past, when he had first come to visit with Phillip during their time at Eton. He had been but four and ten, and she a young girl with a new fascination.

Even then, she found herself dreaming of what their future might be. Despite her innocence, she believed that one day she would grow up to marry this man. They were far too young to understand it fully, but still, she yearned for him. "Theo," she spoke his name as if it were a benediction, for indeed it was to her. "I did not expect to see you."

His ready smile made her heart skip a beat.

"How could I stay away on such a momentous occasion?"

"And what would that be?" she asked, though she knew precisely what he meant. She could not resist teasing him.

"It is your birthday, is it not?" He lifted a brow. "If I am mistaken, do inform me immediately." He held out a small box and waved it in the air. "For if I am wrong, I must return this at once. It would not do for you to receive a gift on a day that is not special."

She leapt to her feet and tried to snatch the box from his hands, but he was much taller, with a greater reach. "Give it to me," Elena demanded.

"But it's not—"

"You know perfectly well it is my birthday," she insisted. "Please, Theo," she begged softly. "Let me have my gift."

"Could I ever deny you anything?" he said, his voice softening. Those blue eyes of his seemed to pierce her very soul. How could she fight the inevitability of her love for him? She could not—and truthfully, she did not wish to. There was nothing she desired more than to belong to Theo. He handed her the box. "I thought of you when I saw it and knew you must have it."

She opened the lid and sighed. Resting on a bed of crushed velvet lay a locket of the finest gold. In the center was a bright ruby fashioned against a round locket, like a star bursting from the center. "It is beautiful," she murmured in awe. "I love it."

"There's a miniature inside," he told her. "Open it."

She undid the clasp, and inside was indeed a miniature. It was of the two of them. "When did you have this done?"

"A while ago," he replied. "It's a good likeness, don't you think?"

She nodded, tracing her fingers over it. They were depicted in profile, gazing at each other with a look of profound affection. She hadn't realized she looked at him in such a way, but she recognized that adoring expression on his handsome face. She had seen it often enough to know it was genuine. "It is perfect," she whispered. "I love you."

"I love you, too." He trailed a finger over her lips. "I wish I could kiss you."

"You can," she encouraged. "I am eight and ten now. We can marry. All you need do is ask my father…"

"Not yet, love," he said gently. "You should have at least one season. Enjoy the pleasures of being a young debutante. You deserve all the world has to offer. Don't worry. I will ask him. How could I not?" He closed his eyes and sighed. "I love you too much to walk away without trying to claim forever with you. But I want so much for you, too."

"I do not want anyone else." Her smile widened. "I can wait though. I have waited this long, have I not?" She stepped closer to him. "We have our whole lives. A few more months will be nothing in comparison to forever."

"Precisely." He took the pendant from the box. "Let me see it upon you. I want to see it lying against your lovely skin."

She allowed him to fasten the necklace around her neck. She touched the starburst, feeling comforted by its presence. It was the finest gift she had ever received. "Thank you," she said. "I don't know if I remembered to say that, but I shall treasure this always."

He leaned down and pressed a soft kiss to her cheek. "I plan to shower you with gifts. This will be but one of many."

"I need no gifts." She gazed into his adoring eyes. "All I need is you."

"But you shall have me and all I can give. I

insist." Theo smiled. "One takes care of those they love, and I love you more than anything."

Elena could scarcely believe her good fortune. This man… "You are almost too perfect to be real."

"Believe in me, darling," he said. "I promise I shall love you all my life. There will be no one else for me." He sighed. "But I must go now. We shall speak again later. There is some estate business that demands my attention. Until later, my love." He pressed a quick kiss to her cheek. "Enjoy your day."

The smile lingered on her face long after he had left, filling her with joy—until the worst happened. She was eight and ten, a woman grown. She could finally marry the man she loved. But fortune was not on her side, and she did not marry Theo.

Her father had other plans. Plans she discovered that very day, not long after Theo left. Her life changed—and not for the better. Yes, she married, but not as she had dreamed. She did not have a season. No, Elena had been sold to an old man desperate for a young wife. Her father had lost a great sum of money to the Earl of Dryden, and the earl generously offered to forgive the debt if Elena were given to him in marriage.

That night, Elena was wed to the Earl of Dryden by special license. She was forced to endure the old earl's lecherous attentions and a marriage bed that left her cold. She'd had a chance at love, and her father had ruined her life instead.

On her birthday, when she had turned eight and ten, she became Elena Wilson, the Countess of Dryden. That new woman was not one to suffer fools. She had to grow up fast, and become a woman not to be trifled with. It was the only way she could survive her new fate. She held her head high and pretended she was exactly where she had always wanted to be—even if it couldn't be further from the truth.

She hated her father. She began to despise most men. And she ensured she never saw the Earl of Northfield again. Her heart could not bear the sight of the only man she would ever love—not while she was bound to a man who repulsed her and subjected her to his loathsome desires. Her life was no longer her own, and if she hoped to survive, she had to bury all her hopes and dreams. She had to close her heart and feel nothing. Most of all, she had to forget what true happiness felt like, for the memory was far too painful. Some things were best left buried...

One

The journey to the Winston estate had taken far longer than Elena would have liked. She did not exactly dislike traveling, but neither did she enjoy it overly much. Her preference would have been to remain in London within the comforts of her townhouse. As a wealthy widow, she could afford to be more discerning in all her endeavors, a freedom she relished. After years of suffering in a distasteful marriage, she was determined never again to be bound in such a union. For her, marriage was a trap she had no intention of falling into a second time.

She had made a wager with her dearest friend, Elias, the Marquess of Savorton, that one of them would fall in love by the end of the house party they were traveling to together. She had foolishly agreed to this wager during a game of piquet. But as Elena had resolved never to give her heart to any man, she fully intended to win. There was only one man she held any affection for anymore, and that was Elias—but it was nothing resembling romantic attachment. He was her one true confidant, a person she trusted implicitly, but only because she knew he harbored no amorous feelings for her either. They were friends, nothing more and nothing less.

The only time she truly felt safe was with Eli. They had been friends since they were children, they're mothers having been close acquaintances. But their friendship had not truly blossomed until after Eli had found her bruised and in pain, following a particularly distressing incident with her late husband. After that they had renewed their friendship and become especially close. That man, her now thankfully dead husband, had hurt her deeply—never in ways visible to others, but in ways that scarred her heart and unseen bodily limbs. Elias had been her refuge during those dark days, and there was nothing Elena wouldn't do for him, even participate in this ludicrous wager. As if she would ever fall in love! She shuddered at the thought.

"The weather has been agreeable, at least,"

Elena remarked, glancing out the carriage window. "It hasn't snowed, and the roads have been passable."

"For that, I am most grateful," Eli replied. "The journey would have been interminable otherwise."

"What sorts of entertainment do you suppose Lady Winston has arranged for us?" Elena tilted her head, meeting his gaze. Their conversation was mundane, a welcome distraction from that infernal wager. "A summer house party offers opportunities for outdoor activities, which are far more challenging in winter."

"Perhaps she will have us build snowmen," Eli said with a smirk. "That could be quite amusing."

Elena raised an eyebrow at the suggestion. What a ridiculous idea… and yet, her lips twitched as she considered it. "Actually, that could be entertaining. If Lady Winston hasn't planned it, perhaps we should suggest it. We could turn it into a competition with judges."

Eli blinked, then frowned. "I'll leave that to you," he replied, his tone indicating the last thing he wished to do was frolic outside building men of snow. "I'm not inclined to propose activities in which I have no interest in participating."

"Oh, but you must," she said, barely containing a

laugh as she looked at her dear friend. "You know the terms of our wager. We're to engage in every activity and cannot hide in our chambers. This was your idea, was it not? Now you must live with the consequences."

He tapped his chin thoughtfully, acknowledging her words. Eli knew she was right and he would not argue her point. Their wager stipulated that they had to partake in all aspects of the house party if they wanted a fair chance at winning.

"I am fully aware of the conditions of our wager," he drawled. "I look forward to our entertainments." His tone, however, suggested anything but enthusiasm. Elena did not blame him; she wasn't particularly looking forward to it, either.

"You work far too hard," she said, a touch of concern coloring her words. She hated how tirelessly Eli worked to keep his family afloat after his father's poor management. "This may sound terrible, but I think once your father passes, your life will be easier. As it is, you run much of the ducal estate's business, yet you still have to answer to him, and he complicates matters."

Eli sighed. "Yes, he does. But he is still my father."

"And you don't wish him dead," Elena

concluded. "I understand. He is a kind man, if somewhat misguided at times." She added softly, thinking of her own father, who had arranged her unfortunate marriage. At least Eli's father had not forced him into misery. Unlike Elena, who had been abandoned by her family, only for her father to reappear after her husband's death, hoping to control her once more. She had quickly disabused him of that notion. She owed that man nothing. Especially her loyalty and allegiance. He'd effectively killed any affection she'd ever had for him.

"Yes," Eli agreed, smiling faintly. "He has been a good father, for the most part."

"Sometimes I wish he had been my father," she said whimsically. "But alas, I had a bully to contend with." She turned to him with a rueful smile. "I haven't spoken to my father in over a year. The last time we met, he attempted to convince me to marry another elderly man."

Eli's brows knitted together. "Why would he do that?"

"He's in debt again, and he thought my marriage to the Viscount of Redding would settle his accounts," she replied with a disdainful wrinkle of her nose. "I would gain nothing from that union except a lesser title." She shuddered. The notion of once again being a pawn in her father's games was abhorrent. "I would have had to endure another elderly husband—no, thank you. If I ever take a lover, he will be young, virile, and skilled in making a woman feel truly desired." She laughed, though her words carried a hint of sadness. She wouldn't take a lover. That would give a man some control over her and she feared letting go and allowing a man to have any sway over her. Even if it was meant to be pleasurable.

"I'm relieved he no longer holds any sway over you," Eli said earnestly.

"As am I." The carriage turned down a long, tree-lined drive that led to the Winston estate. "Oh, thank heavens," she exclaimed. "We have arrived."

"Indeed," Eli replied.

A thrill of anticipation stirred within her. Soon, the festivities would begin, and Elena had every intention of helping her dear friend find a worthy match. Eli deserved a wife who would cherish him. Perhaps love was elusive for her, but she would not rest until Eli found happiness.

THEODORE JONES, THE EARL OF NORTHFIELD, LEANED back against his carriage, feeling a rare sense of reluctance. He was headed to a house party—a gathering he would normally avoid. Theo had little patience for societal functions that offered him nothing he desired. He did not wish to marry, nor did he care to engage in tedious discussions about fashion or the weather. He especially did not relish gambling, excessive drinking, or pretending to be carefree.

Theo no longer knew how to be something as whimsical as carefree...

He had celebrated his thirtieth year a few months earlier, and he'd had a hard look at his life and the disappointments that had come to pass.

Theo had fallen in love years earlier and he had found that once he had been denied that happiness he had no taste for marriage or children. He had no desire to secure his legacy, for he had no interest in leaving anything behind. As far as he was concerned it could pass on to some distant cousin of his and they could worry about begetting heirs.

Yet here he was, enroute to a Christmas house party...

Why? Because of a brief yet intriguing letter from the Marquess of Savorton. Theo hoped to have dealings with Savorton Shipping and he held a great deal of respect for the marquess, who had built his own empire despite his father's objections. Savorton was intelligent, resilient, and, Theo suspected, fiercely loyal to his friends. And Theo was certain that Savorton's loyalty extended to Elena—the one woman Theo had loved and lost because of the machinations of her family.

Theo pulled out the letter once more, reading it in the hopes that it would somehow provide clarity:

> Northfield,
> Lady Winston is hosting a Christmas house party. You were sent an invitation. Accept it and take this one final chance with the woman who holds your heart.
> —Savorton

THEO HAD NEVER SHARED HIS FEELINGS FOR ELENA WITH Savorton, yet it seemed her confidant had discerned the truth. How had he known? What had Elena revealed? Theo's mind whirled with questions, but there was only one way to find answers. That was why he traveled to Lady Winston's estate, why he had accepted an invitation he would otherwise have ignored. Elena would be there, and he would seize this chance to rekindle their love.

Closing his eyes, Theo took a deep breath. For Elena... for the possibility of a future with her... He would endure anything, even a Christmas house party and all its associated pleasantries.

Nothing would keep him from her, not this time. Theo fully intended to woo and win her heart once more. Elena was his everything, and he'd convince her of that fact. He had to, because he could not fathom living out his life without her by his side. He'd have her any way she'd allow. Even if it meant living in sin, and never having her as his wife. For her he'd consider everything and offer any allowance. Because without her, nothing else mattered.

Two

Elena smiled as she wandered through the hall. She was searching the house. Not for a place to hide, and Eli would have accused her, but for someone in particular. She had noticed that Eli had taken an interest in one of the ladies in attendance. Oh, he had tried to hide his interest, but he had not succeeded. Elena knew him too well. No one else would have noticed, but she had, and Elena would definitely take advantage of it. She wanted her friend to find love, and if this lady was the one that had caught his attention... Well, then she would ensure that the lady returned that attention.

Which was why she was currently wandering around the house in search of that lady. She wanted to introduce herself, and then become fast friends with her. Once she located her she would insert herself, as much as she was able to, into the girls life. Then she would encourage her to spend time with Eli and hopefully they would fall in love and live happily-ever-after. If such an ending existed... Elena had her doubts considering her own less than tasteful venture in marriage.

Elena entered a room and barely kept a grin to herself as she noticed the dark haired beauty sitting alone. She'd found her. Thank heaven. Now for her to begin her machinations. The lady glanced up and met her gaze. She was truly a lovely young woman and she could see why Eli would be intrigued by her. The question, of course, was she worthy of her friend. It was time to ascertain that very thing. Today she wore a gown of emerald silk that matched her lovely eyes. "Good afternoon," The young woman greeted Elena.

Elena beamed at her. "I don't believe we have been introduced," she began. "I am Lady Dryden." She waited for the young woman to address her. She wanted to be more forward, but didn't wish to scare the poor thing. Undoubtedly, the woman wouldn't be accustomed to such behavior. Elena was used to being more brash and bold. She'd had to be that way. It was how she survived after her husband had beaten her. She would have turned into a sniveling coward otherwise.

"It is a pleasure to make your acquaintance, Lady Dryden." The young woman said, then smiled at her. "I am Lady Gabriella St. Giles." She had seemed so lost in thought. Was she thinking about Eli as she sat alone in this room?

Elena nodded at her. "Do you mind if I join you?" She moved closer to Lady Gabriella with the intention of sitting regardless of what she agreed to.

As she made her way across the room she studied Lady Gabriella. She had luscious dark locks and brilliant green eyes. Her heart shaped face and full lips were features that most other young ladies would be envious of, and wish they could have. But features like hers were not so easy to come by or emulate. Elena wouldn't want to be just like her, but she could see why others might wish to. Those ladies were not comfortable in their own skin.

"Of course," Lady Gabriella told her. "I'm just lost in my own thoughts." She gestured toward a chair near the settee. "Please sit. I could use the company." Elena went to the settee and settled into the seat. She was prepared to stay as long as necessary. She had a plan and she would see it through.

"Are you experiencing a bit of the doldrums?" Elena asked. "The entertainments thus far have been tedious." She suspected all of the entertainments would be much the same. Not that she'd been that much of a participant. They had not been at Lady Winston's long enough to enjoy much of what had been planned for the guests.

"It's been all right," Lady Gabriella answered, though she did not sound enthusiastic. "My friend has taken a liking to one of the gentlemen in attendance and, therefore, left me to my own devices. Not that I mind." Lady Gabriella shrugged. "The gentleman in question has to be far more appealing than her mother."

Elena laughed. It was a rich throaty laugh. How interesting... She could not wait to learn more. "Am I to understand that her mother is insufferable?" She sighed. Elena had been around many unbearable ladies since she'd been married. No doubt Lady Gabriella's friend's mother was comparable to them. "I have my own experiences with people similar to that. I feel for your friend."

"Clara will be all right," Lady Gabriella explained. "Mrs. Adams seems to like her potential suitor and is encouraging the match. If it goes somewhere, then she'll be free to do as she pleases." She frowned. "Well, it might not be as simple as that. Some marriage are not so wonderful are they?"

"Quite true," Elena agreed, remembering her days as a young wife. Her marriage had not been her choosing, but still, she'd had hope it wouldn't be that terrible. Oh, how wrong he'd been. Those were memories she wished she could forget. Though that was unlikely. Nothing would completely wash them from her mind. Sometimes the more horrid ones sneaked in when she least expected it, and she struggled to breathe as they beat her internally. Almost as if her dreadful husband still drew breath. "But that is far too serious a discussion for a lovely afternoon. She leaned on the arm of the chair. Tell me about yourself."

"What would you like to know?" Lady Gabriella asked. She stared at Elena expectantly. "There is nothing exciting about me." Now that wasn't the truth. The very fact that Eli had taken an interest in her was enough for Elena. She would be engrossing even without that to recommend her, but Eli's fascination with her was the reason Elena had come to find her. So she would stay and she would learn all she could about the girl.

"That cannot be the truth," Elena said. She had to make the girl talk more. But how? Then an idea struck her and she added, "Or you would not have caught the attention of my dear friend." Surely that would be enough to make Lady Gabriella curious. She had to spark that within her so they could move forward. Elena had to push them toward a relationship and hopefully they would then fall madly in love.

Lady Gabriella narrowed her gaze. "Pardon me," she began. "What friend?" The girl must not know of Elena's friendship with Eli. How much did she even know about him? Elena would have to prod a little there as well.

"Lord Savorton," Elena said, and then lifted her lips upward into a confident smile. "You are acquainted with him, are you not?" No young lady would forget meeting the Marquess of Savorton. He was handsome, titled, and charming. She waited for Lady Gabriella to confirm that she'd met Eli. From there she could move the conversation in the direction she wished for it to go.

"I met him in the conservatory," Lady Gabriella admitted. "But that hardly means he likes me. He was polite, nothing more." She frowned. Almost as if she couldn't believe that Eli might find her attractive. How interesting. Elena didn't think that Lady Gabriella would be so unassuming or modest. How could she not believe that Eli wouldn't be interested in her?

"Ah," Elena said. "I had wondered…" Her voice trailed off as her eyes glazed over as if she was lost in thought. This girl was quite naive. Much like Elena had once been. Back when she believed in love, and had willingly given her heart away. That young girl she'd once been no longer existed. She snapped out of it and met Lady Gabriella's gaze. She couldn't allow herself to revisit her past. It would not aid her now. "He pays attention to you."

"I doubt that." She nibbled on her bottom lip. Lady Gabriella doubted a man as handsome and titled as Eli wouldn't want her. Why was that?

"Oh, trust me, he does." Elena tapped her fingers lightly on the arm of her chair. "He is subtle about it, but I know him better than anyone. He's interested in you." She leaned a little closer. "Would you like to know him better?" She had to entice the young woman into accepting her help. Somehow she would bring the two of them together.

"Why would you be willing to aid me in this?" Lady Gabriella scrunched her eyebrows together in confusion. "Isn't he your friend?" Elena could tell her about the wager, but she doubted that she'd understand. She might even be offended by it. That was not the most optimal way to handle this situation.

"That is precisely why," she said, and flipped her hand dismissively. "I don't expect you to understand. Eli—Savorton," Elena corrected herself. "And I have been friends since we were children. He's been struggling for sometime now to keep his family estates together, and now that he has succeeded he fears everything will somehow be snatched away from him. He's miserable and doesn't even realize it." She tilted her head to the side. "He doesn't notice women. They are not worth his attention when everything else is at stake, but you, my dear, are different. I want to encourage that if it is possible."

"You're only seeking his happiness?" Lady Gabriella's voice held a hint of skepticism in it. Elena couldn't fault her for not believing her. In her place she'd question it all as well. For that she respected the woman a whole lot more. That showed she had some intelligence, and Elena appreciated that more than anything.

"Exactly," Elena said. "And I do think you might make him happy." At least she hoped she would... Happiness could be elusive and fleeting. No one knew that better than Elena did. Her happiness had been far too brief, and painful to remember even now.

"I might not make him happy," Lady Gabriella told her. "You can't force something that is not there." Truer words had never been spoken before… Nothing could be forced. Well that wasn't exactly the truth was it? Her father had forced her into a marriage. True love and happiness couldn't be though. That was what Elena wanted for Eli.

"Are you telling me that it would take some effort on your part to feel something for the marquess?" Elena lifted a brow. "Because I've seen you watching him, too. You're not even sly about it as he has been." Lady Gabriella didn't fool her. She was attracted to Eli, and that attraction was completely understandable.

"I cannot do it," Lady Gabriella told her. "I won't scheme for any reason, and I don't need to."

Lady Dryden's smile grew. She didn't want her to scheme. All she wanted from Lady Gabriella was for her to be open to the possibility of something with Eli. That wasn't too much to ask. At least she did not think it was… "I like you. You'll do."

Elena didn't elaborate on that because right then Eli entered the room with the one man she'd been avoiding for years. He was as handsome as she remembered. His dark hair curled a little against his nape and those eyes of his... She had always been drawn to those beautiful blue eyes. She tore her gaze away from him and turned her attention to Eli. She glared at him. How could he have done this to her? He knew how she felt about the Earl of Northfield. Her smile faded as she turned and met the earl's gaze and fought the urge to flee. He couldn't really be there. Standing next to Eli and staring at her as if he still loved her. It couldn't be possible... God help her, she couldn't handle this. Pain shot through her and stabbed directly through her aching heart. She was not prepared for this.

Three

Eli stood in the entryway with the Earl of Northfield at his side. Elena stared at them, unable to form words. Her throat went dry, and all coherent thought fled. Her mind blanked as dread filled her. This couldn't be happening. It *could not* be happening. But it was. He was here, standing next to her closest friend as if this were not a monumental occasion. As if no time had passed and it was perfectly acceptable for him to arrive at Lady Winston's house party—as if they had never meant anything to each other, and she had never loved him with all the innocence of youth.

"We're not interrupting, are we?" Eli asked, attempting to appear nonchalant. Elena was not fooled. She saw through his pretense. They would have words later, and he would not like what she had to say.

"Not at all," Elena replied, narrowing her gaze and studying Eli shrewdly. She smiled slyly and added, "Please, join us." Her tone conveyed what she had left unsaid. Good. He ought to be wary.

Lord Northfield took the chair closest to Elena. Her breath caught. He was so close. Too close. She couldn't very well demand that he remove himself and find somewhere else to sit; that would be the height of rudeness. Not that she was above being rude on occasion, but she required a *very* good reason to act in such a manner.

Eli glanced at the remaining open seat, which was on the settee next to Lady Gabriella. Without looking in Lady Gabriella's direction, he focused his attention on Elena. "Lord Northfield is interested in doing business with Savorton Shipping. We have been discussing the possibility since his arrival earlier today."

"How wonderful for him," Elena replied coolly, pointedly avoiding looking in the earl's direction. She was doing her best to pretend she didn't know him, though he surely knew better. She had caught Theo looking at her with a hint of longing in those striking blue eyes of his. She could not allow him to realize his effect on her. "I trust your discussion is going well." Somehow, she managed to keep all emotion from her voice.

"It is," Northfield replied. "Lady Dryden," he said softly. Reluctantly, Elena looked at him. "I trust you are well." *Damn him...* Why did he still have to be so blessedly kind—and so handsome? Painfully handsome, in fact, as it hurt to look at him.

"Is there any reason I wouldn't be?" she replied, her tone verging on petulance. Without waiting for an answer, she turned to Lady Gabriella. "Do you play cards, dear?" She had to keep her distance from the earl. Somehow, she would remain aloof.

"I cannot say I have any skill at card games," Lady Gabriella admitted. "I have had no reason to learn."

"Then we shall rectify that." Elena grinned. "We have enough here for a game of Faro." She turned to the earl. "Are you willing to join us, my lord?" Then she glanced at Eli. "He'll play. He can never turn down a game of cards." *What in heaven's name was she doing?* This was an invitation she shouldn't have extended. Clearly, she was losing her senses. Now, she would have to spend an evening playing Faro with the earl, Eli, and Lady Gabriella.

"You're implying I am a consummate gambler,

darling." Eli shook his head with a mock frown. "What will they think of me?"

"They'll think that you enjoy cards." Elena shrugged. Eli did enjoy cards; they both did, and they were both skilled. "That doesn't mean you have a dreadful gambling habit." Her lips twitched as she allowed herself a grin. "Besides, a good gamble can be quite enjoyable when done correctly." She meant it as a reminder of their wager.

Eli turned his attention to Lady Gabriella. "Do you wish to learn how to play Faro?" *Good.* He was focusing on the lady who had caught his interest. She might have foolishly arranged this card game, but that didn't mean she couldn't use it to her advantage. She would push Eli toward Lady Gabriella and simultaneously do her best to pretend she wasn't still affected by the Earl of Northfield.

Lady Gabriella tilted her head thoughtfully before answering. "I wouldn't mind if you're willing to teach me."

"I'm sure we'll all be happy to assist until you grasp the basics. Besides," Eli added, "this will be for fun only. There's no reason to risk gambling with a novice. That would hardly be fair."

"Then let's play," Lady Gabriella said, sounding

as though she truly wished to learn. *Excellent.* Elena suppressed a smile.

"Perfect," Elena said in an agreeable tone. "We shall meet in the game room in an hour. I'll see to refreshments and ensure we have a proper deck of cards." She stood and turned to Lady Gabriella. "Don't worry, dear. You're in excellent hands with me." She winked, catching Eli's glare. He knew her too well not to realize she was up to something. Well, he'd best be prepared.

"I'm not concerned," Gabriella replied, meeting Elena's gaze without flinching. "I do learn quickly and doubt I'll need much assistance. Perhaps we can make the game more interesting once I understand the rules."

"I like you," Elena said with a smile. She turned to Eli. "I trust an hour is sufficient for you and Lord Northfield?" She still didn't look directly at Theo; she couldn't. If she did, she might betray more than she intended.

"Plenty," Eli assured her. "Go on and make the arrangements. We'll join you shortly."

With those words, Elena left the room. She had plans to make and a game to set up. By the end of the evening, she hoped Eli would be much closer to falling for Lady Gabriella. As for the earl... her former love... She would keep him firmly in the past. There was no second chance for them. She had abandoned those dreams long ago. Elena no longer believed in love, and her heart could not bear the risk of reopening old wounds. No, she did not want Theo. She did not want *any* man.

THEO DREW IN A DEEP, FORTIFYING BREATH. THAT HAD not gone well at all. Elena had looked right through him, as though he were nothing. Did she hate him now? What did she want from him? He didn't know what she expected of him; she had pushed him aside as if they had never meant a thing to each other, as if they had never been in love, as if they had never been the center of each other's world. Did she not understand how much he still ached for her? Had she ever truly loved him?

Was he fooling himself?

Perhaps he should give in and go home. As much as he loved her—he did have some pride, after all. Did he truly wish to lay his heart at her feet and hope she still wanted him? Was he that much of a besotted fool?

Yes. Yes, he absolutely was. Everything came

down to one simple truth: he loved her. He had always loved her. This was his last chance to have her in his life, and therefore, he had to try to win her heart again. If she no longer loved him... Well, then he would let her go. Every dream and hope he'd held would float away on the wind. It would hurt, but if that was all he had, then he would walk away. He knew in his heart that she was the only woman for him. If he gave up without fighting for her, what did that say about him? He would prove to her that he was exactly what she needed, and more importantly, he would prove that she could trust him.

"Are you going to play cards?" Savorton asked.

Theo glanced in his direction. Savorton had just returned to the room. The other lady... What was her name? Gabriella? He couldn't be certain. Her name hardly mattered. What mattered was that she had excused herself to prepare for their game of cards, leaving him alone with Savorton. Now, he could speak freely, without either of the ladies present. "I intend to," he replied, tilting his head to the side. "Is there a reason I should not?"

Savorton shook his head. "No. You absolutely should play."

"She seems so different..." There had been a pain in her gaze that she had tried to mask. Theo wished he could erase it, but he knew that was impossible. "I wish..."

"What do you wish?" Savorton asked.

"So many things..." He wished he could go back in time and take her away before she'd married the Earl of Dryden. He would have taken her to Scotland and eloped with her. Then she'd have been safe with him. She would never have endured the suffering that had turned her into a woman who now looked through him as if he meant nothing to her. Perhaps he could have saved her from the agony of a marriage that had clearly been brutal. He had so many regrets. "But wishing never helped anyone."

Savorton nodded. "You do know it will be an uphill battle?"

"I do," Theo answered, turning to meet the marquess's gaze. "But nothing worth having has ever been easy, has it? She's worth everything, and I will do whatever it takes. When it's all said and done, she's the only thing that matters."

The marquess nodded. "Do you know what her marriage was like?"

Theo shook his head. He had heard things but tried not to listen. He hated the thought of her being mistreated and himself powerless to help. The law had been on her husband's side, and if Theo had known anything with certainty, he would have acted, though they both would have paid a hefty price. "I can only imagine."

"Perhaps it is best you do not know," Savorton said softly. "I know far more than I would like." He walked over to a nearby bar, poured two snifters of brandy, brought a glass over to Theo, and took a sip from his own. "It's enough to give a person nightmares—and I didn't even live through it." He took another sip, then closed his eyes. "He hurt her, and I don't mean just emotionally, though he did that as well."

Theo swallowed hard, gritting his teeth. God, he didn't want to know this. But perhaps he should listen and heed every detail. He did not want to bungle this, and he would if he didn't understand everything. "I wish I could raise him from the dead and kill him all over again."

"You and me both," Savorton said. "I found her after a particularly brutal night. She was..." He shook his head. "If the man hadn't gone and fallen off his horse that same night, breaking his own neck, I would have killed him myself. The bastard met his end too swiftly—and not nearly as painful as it should have been."

"She's free of him now, though..." Theo lifted his

glass and took a long, deep drink. The brandy burned as it traveled down his throat.

"She isn't, though." The marquess set his glass down. "Oh, he's dead, and he can't add any new bruises, but his cruelty still haunts her. She won't allow herself to become involved with a man. Not even to take a lover. She's still... skittish."

"What do you want me to do?" If she was afraid of men, she'd never admit she might still love him. Was he doing her a disservice by attending this house party? Should he leave her alone?

"You cannot allow her to recoil from the world and become a shadow of herself." Savorton sighed. "You're here to bring her back to the living. She's half-dead, though she would deny it." He met Theo's gaze. "I know you once loved her..."

"I still love her," he said adamantly. "I wanted to marry her. Her damnable father prevented it."

"Good," Savorton said. "Then fight for her. Don't let her push you away. She still loves you, though she will deny that too. Do not give up on her. She needs you."

Theo considered the marquess's words, then nodded. "But if this is too much for her, if she truly cannot bear it, I will walk away. I refuse to add to her suffering."

The marquess nodded. "That will have to be enough." He smiled. "Now, let us join the ladies for a game of Faro. I believe it might prove rather entertaining."

He hoped so. Theo wanted nothing more than to be near Elena, and he hoped he could win her heart again. The marquess thought she still loved him, but Theo would not take that on faith. He would find out for himself and, in time, prove to her that there was nothing to fear. They had loved each other once, and he damn well still loved her. He would start with this game of cards and follow her lead from there. The more she let him in, the better. This had to be on her terms—or not at all.

Four

Elena still could not fathom why she had thought arranging a game of cards—or rather, a lesson on how to play cards for Lady Gabriella—would be such a brilliant idea. Clearly, she had lost her wits. Not that she didn't enjoy cards; on the contrary, she loved them—immensely. But not when the Earl of Northfield would be among the players. He would be a distraction she simply could not afford. Unfortunately, there was no conceivable way to exclude him from the game. She would have to find a way to manage his presence or somehow pretend he wasn't there. An impossible task if she ever heard one...

Would that even be possible? She doubted it. She was too attuned to him for such a feat. Elena could never act as if he did not exist. Perhaps it would be wiser to engage with him as little as possible. Her task now was to avoid acknowledging how much he still affected her. Somehow, she would summon the strength to endure the evening spent in his company over a game of cards. Elena believed in her skills at pretense. She'd honed them enough over the years of her marriage. It was a tool she had needed to survive, and if she was anything it was a survivor.

Drawing a deep breath, she straightened her shoulders. There was no avoiding the inevitable. It had been her idea, after all, and she would have to see it through—lest she appear the fool she already felt like. Elena strolled into the game room, sighing upon finding herself the first to arrive. How was that possible? She had delayed as long as was decent before heading to the game room, and now she was forced to wait for the others to join her. She supposed she could make certain everything was in order so they could begin the game as soon as the party gathered. It was to her advantage to do so, and she was mercenary enough to use whatever arsenal was at her disposal.

They could choose from various games, but she favored Faro. It was one of the simplest games of chance to learn, and she suspected Lady Gabriella might find it enjoyable. The odds were nearly even, and they wouldn't need partners; one of them could act as the dealer. Elena fully intended to take that role, maintaining control over the game and limiting her interaction with the others. She would have to pay attention to each person equally and not favor any of them. That would be enough for her to keep the earl at a distance. A necessary part of the upcoming interaction she'd lay heavily on throughout the game.

As she set the table with the necessary items, the remaining three entered almost simultaneously, with Lord Northfield trailing last. Lady Gabriella and Eli walked in together, as if they had come side-by-side. Eli seemed in high spirits around Lady Gabriella. Surely this meant her dear friend had found someone he could grow fond of—if he allowed himself the sentiment. She certainly hoped he would; that wager of theirs had compelled her to arrange this foolhardy gathering. Once Eli fell in love she could depart the house party and never look back.

"I am so glad you three could join me," she greeted with a pleasant smile, then turned to Lady Gabriella. "Come," she gestured to the table, "sit here, and I shall give you a quick lesson and explain the rules."

Lady Gabriella moved over and took a seat. Meanwhile, Lord Northfield and Eli lingered behind, apparently deep in conversation. The sight made Elena slightly uneasy, but she held her tongue. Let them talk; if Eli was scheming—highly likely—she would deal with it later. Her priority now was Lady Gabriella. "The first thing to know," Elena began, "is that you are playing for yourself, and the cards will be dealt from this box." She tapped it lightly, then proceeded to explain the rules of Faro. Lady Gabriella was an excellent pupil absorbing all the details with ease. Now she had to encourage the other two to join them so they could play. She had avoided the inevitable as long as she could. Now it was time to face them all and play Faro.

"We're ready," she called out. "If the two of you have finished your discussion, I would like to start the game."

Eli nodded. "We'll be right there."

She threw him a look of reproach, to which he only laughed. Insolent rakehell... She sighed, taking her seat at the table. Studying Lady Gabriella, Elena pondered whether she ought to probe further about Eli. Would it seem too forward to encourage Lady

Gabriella to spend time with him again? She was on the verge of saying something when Eli and Lord Northfield finally joined them, with Eli seating himself beside Lady Gabriella and Lord Northfield taking the chair to his left.

"Now that you both have been so kind as to join us," Elena said with a touch of censure in her tone, "I shall begin dealing the game." She fixed Eli with a meaningful look. "I expect you to assist Lady Gabriella through the first few rounds to help her learn the game."

"We aren't playing for real stakes, I assume?" Eli asked.

"Not at present," Elena clarified. "Though perhaps at a future game, once Lady Gabriella is more confident in her skills." Something Elena would likely be present to witness.

"Excellent," Eli said, running a hand through his dark hair before flashing his roguish smile—the very one that tended to set many hearts aflutter. Fortunately for her, Elena was not one of those women who fell at his feet. "Then let us begin."

The Earl of Northfield remained silent, neither contributing nor questioning. He merely sat there, observing, as though gauging her reaction. It saddened Elena to realize how far they'd drifted apart because of her forced marriage. Theo... her Theo. She nearly sighed. She must return to thinking of him as Lord Northfield. It was the only way she could keep her heart at a safe distance. The very sight of him still brought a pang to her chest.

Elena turned to the card box and commenced the game. So long as they were playing, she could pretend this was not an agony. She moved through the motions with practiced ease, as if she felt nothing at all. But that, she knew, was the greatest lie of all—the truth was she felt far, far too much...

Theo did not want to play cards. But he had gone to the game room to do just that. Even his earlier conversation with Lord Savorton had been more pretense than anything he genuinely wished to discuss. His sole reason for attending the house party was Elena, and she was doing everything in her power to ignore his presence. He didn't blame her, even if it gnawed at his patience.

He played Faro and helped Lady Gabriella grasp the game's mechanics, yet remembered very little of it. Not because the game lacked entertainment or Lady Gabriella lacked charm and wit, but because nothing shone as brightly for him as Elena. All else faded into insignificance. How could it not? She had been his everything for too long.

When the game ended and Lady Gabriella departed with Lord Savorton, Theo remained behind. Elena still did not acknowledge him, focusing instead on tidying the cards and returning them to the box. He watched her, noting how she kept her distance and her demeanor chilly. It stung more than he cared to admit. He wanted her to see him again, to look at him with the warmth she once had. But she didn't, and the ache in his chest was like a wound reopening.

"Elena," he said softly.

She froze, her hand resting on the card box. Her back was to him, so he couldn't see her face—only the gentle curves of her form and the rich auburn of her hair. He wanted to loosen her elegant chignon and watch her locks spill down her back, as he'd imagined countless times. The ache in him only grew sharper, a longing that refused to fade.

"Are you going to ignore me for all of Christmastide?" Theo asked, his tone quiet but firm.

Slowly, she turned to face him. Her eyes held a look that chilled him—a mixture of pity and resignation. Another blow to his heart. Did she truly feel nothing for him now? Was she lost to him forever? He couldn't accept that. Not yet. If, by the end of Christmastide, she still wanted nothing to do with him, he would walk away. But he had to try.

"I haven't ignored you," Elena replied, her tone stern. "We played Faro, did we not? Or have you already forgotten?"

"You know precisely what I mean," he said, his voice hardening. Theo couldn't let her evade him. Not now.

"Do I?" She raised a brow. "And how would you know one way or the other?"

"Because I know you." He held her gaze steadily. She was putting on a mask of indifference, but there were cracks in her armor. He saw it in her slight flinch when he spoke her name. "It's time you stopped pushing me away."

"I didn't realize I had," she replied, turning away to adjust the cards for what felt like the hundredth time. "What is it you think you know, Lord Northfield?"

"I didn't realize you'd stopped using my given name," he said softly. "Am I no longer someone you know, Elena?"

She stiffened again. "I ceased being that girl you knew when I married Lord Dryden." She turned back to him, her gaze steely. "That girl had to grow up, faster than she'd have liked. Life isn't a fairy tale—not the sort with a happy ending. The ones that have the harsher endings and diabolical evil—that's what I've had in my life. That's the life I've had."

He shook his head. "I wish—"

"Wishing never helped anyone." Her voice was so cold it was like ice on his skin. He suppressed a shiver. "Don't offer me platitudes. I survived. That is enough."

"Is it?" he asked, raising a brow. "Because there is more to life than merely surviving."

She stepped closer to the table, and Theo rose to his feet. She was achingly beautiful, and he wanted nothing more than to wrap her in his arms, to soothe away the hurt he saw lingering in her eyes. But he knew some wounds were too deep to be so easily healed.

"I would not be here if I had not learned to survive," she said evenly. "I'm grateful for the strength I found. I am sorry you do not seem to appreciate the woman I am today. But I cannot change. Not even for you."

"What is that supposed to mean?" Theo said, his voice gentle. He didn't want to change her; he only wanted to care for her, to love her. "I never asked "

"You did not need to." She met his gaze without wavering. "I can see what you want from me. But I can't be that person for you. I can't be anything for anyone."

Theo swallowed hard. He had not anticipated how difficult this would be. He had thought he could simply tell her he loved her, and all would be well. That they would reclaim the love they had promised each other long ago. Now he saw how naive that hope had been.

"You deserve more than the life you have had," he said, his tone soft. "I may not be what you want anymore, but you are still the woman I gave my heart to. Even if you no longer believe that."

With those words, he turned and left the room. Theo needed time alone to gather his thoughts. This was his last chance to win her heart, and he couldn't fail. He simply couldn't.

Five

Theo strolled into the library, though he wasn't entirely certain why he'd bothered. It wasn't as if reading would help settle the tumultuous thoughts and emotions that tore through him. He had come to the house party with one purpose, and that very purpose had spurned him without allowing him the chance to express his desires. Perhaps it was selfish of him, wanting her so deeply and expecting her to welcome him back with open arms. She'd been through something harrowing, and he had no rights where she was concerned, even if he wished he did.

He stared at the shelves, but none of the tomes came into focus. They blurred before his eyes, as ephemeral as his chances of winning Elena's heart once more. Maybe he should leave her be. She hadn't been pleased to see him, after all. Did he even have the right to unsettle her life like this? To him, she would always be perfect. He knew he had to treat her as a precious gift, for loving someone meant putting their needs first, above his own selfish desires.

"I've been searching for you," Lord Savorton said, pulling Theo from his brooding thoughts.

Theo turned to meet the marquess's gaze. "Have you? And for what purpose?" He wasn't certain he wished to know why Savorton had sought him out. He'd been too engrossed in his own self loathing and failure where Elena was concerned.

Savorton leaned against the doorframe, arms crossed, studying him. He was silent for a moment, as if weighing his words. Theo had come to know him well enough over the past few months with their business dealings. Though they hadn't had much opportunity to socialize in previously, he knew Savorton and Elena had always been close. She'd spoken fondly of him before, and he could see that her loyalty was reciprocated by the marquess. If only Elena had that much faith in Theo. He'd truly be a fortunate man then.

Savorton sighed. "You're not leaving."

How had even known that Theo was considering doing just that? "I didn't plan to." He gave the marquess a wry smile. He hadn't planned on leaving. At least not until morning. "It's too late to depart and I would rather not travel the roads at this late hour."

The marquess shook his head. "I didn't mean immediately." He moved further into the room, a serious expression settling over his features. "One inconsequential card game and you're ready to walk away. Was your love so fragile that it can't withstand a little strain?"

Theo clenched his jaw, fighting the urge to deliver a sharp retort. The implication that his love for Elena was anything but genuine stung. "I can't make her love me." He clenched his fingers into his fast at his side. He wanted to strike that too pretty face of the marquess and make Savorton feel the pain that spread over him.

"Then it's fortunate that you don't need to." Savorton's gaze was piercing. He shook his head as if he couldn't believe how stupid Theo was acting. "She already loves you. Her feelings are not the issue. It's her fear of what that love could mean that you must contend with."

Theo closed his eyes, breathing deeply. He

wanted to believe him. "You make it sound so simple," he murmured. It was anything but that…

"Because it is," he told him. "Oh I don't think it will be easy." He kept his gaze on Theo as he spoke. "Simple and easy are vastly different things," Savorton replied. "The question is how far you'll go to make her trust in your love again, to help her see that what you offer isn't a threat but a promise. She wants you. Elena has always wanted you. But her marriage to that brute has damaged her faith in love itself. It's up to you to restore it."

He knew that Savorton was correct. Theo had always known that. But he also didn't want to make Elena feel as if she had to choose him. All he wanted was her to find happiness again. He swallowed hard—even if that happiness did not include him. "I won't leave her."

"Good," Savorton said, satisfaction evident in his tone. "And I'm here to help however I can. She won't thank me for my interference, and she'll be difficult, but that's a part of her strength. Elena hasn't survived this long without being fierce."

Theo smiled, feeling a tinge of warmth at the marquess's loyalty to her. "That's one of the many things I adore about her. She's stronger than she knows."

Savorton nodded, his tone softening. "True, but she's also more fragile than she lets on. I won't allow her to be hurt again. I believe you're what she needs, that she has always loved you. She has always loved you and it's time she remembered that she needs you, and the comfort she can only find with you in her life."

Theo prayed that was true. He dreamed of a life together, one filled with love, trust, and devotion. Every part of him belonged to Elena. He met Savorton's steady gaze. "I promise I'll do whatever it takes to protect her. I don't know if we'll find our way back to each other, but she is my priority. I won't ruin the peace she's gained since Dryden's death."

Savorton nodded. "Then that is enough. I'll leave you to ponder that, though I hope this conversation has given you clarity." With that, the marquess turned and left the room.

Theo didn't need a book to pass the time. What he wanted was to find Elena and have a moment alone with her. Perhaps he had been too gentle, too cautious. She might need a slight push to see the future they could share. With newfound resolve, he left the library, determined to find the love of his life —and perhaps, if he was fortunate, he might finally break through the walls she had built around her heart.

Elena took a deep breath, reminding herself that she was free to make her own decisions. She wasn't sure why she needed the reminder—it simply seemed necessary in moments of emotional turmoil. Having the Earl of Northfield in residence at the same Christmastide house party likely contributed to her unease. Not that he had done anything to warrant the apprehension that filled her; it was more her own uncertainty. The earl had always been the kindest of men, and even now, when she was being so bloody difficult, he honored her wishes.

The problem, of course, was that she no longer knew what she truly wanted. She had once thought her desires were clear, but her fears had taken over. Elena blamed her late husband for the doubt that kept her from moving forward. Once, she had desperately wanted to be Theo's wife, to share her life with him. But that dream had been dashed before it ever had a chance. Now that she could have that future, she could not allow herself the luxury.

Elena was…damaged.

She could not be the kind of wife Theo deserved. He needed someone whole, someone he could be proud to call his own. She couldn't shake the shadow of her past. Her husband had abused her daily, and when his attempts to impregnate her failed, the abuse only worsened. She feared she might never bear children. The lord knew Dryden had done his best to get her with child. He'd used her roughly, day after day, and when she had fought back, his cruelty grew darker, leaving her battered and bruised. It had been better to allow him to use her. She had endured, and kept her dissent to herself. Those years with him had altered her in ways that she could never fully express. She had a far darker outlook on life now.

Theo should have a wife who could give him heirs and who didn't shudder at the idea of lying with a man. She had always acted as if she'd taken lovers, but she hadn't; the thought of intimacy filled her with distaste. No, she could never be what Theo needed. He deserved so much more than she could ever offer him. Somehow she would have to make him understand.

"This is the last place I expected to find you," Theo said as he entered the conservatory.

Elena closed her eyes, reminding herself to

breathe. She could endure this. Theo would never hurt her. He was as trustworthy as Eli—her dear friend. Slowly, she turned to face him, her expression carefully impassive, concealing just how much he still affected her. "Were you looking for me?" she asked.

"I was," he replied, strolling further into the conservatory. He stopped by the orange tree, inhaling its fragrance with a smile. "These smell wonderful."

"Lady Winston is quite the connoisseur," Elena replied. "She adores oranges. I believe there's a lemon tree somewhere as well." This was a silly conversation, but at least it held the illusion of safety.

"Is there?" His smile widened. "I suppose they come in handy when making punch for guests." Theo moved closer. "But I didn't come here to discuss lemons and oranges."

She had hoped to avoid a serious conversation, but clearly, he had other plans. "But they are such interesting plants." Her lips twitched in a faint smile. "And delicious too."

"I won't disagree," he said, "but I'd much rather talk about you."

She sighed, realizing her final attempt to steer him off course had failed. "I'm not open to that discussion," she replied, her smile fading. "Some things are best left in the past."

"I disagree," he said gently. He reached out, brushing his thumb over her cheek. "But it isn't the past I wish to discuss with you."

She was taken aback. What could he want, if not to speak of how their future had been stolen by her father's choices? Without her father's gambling, she would have married Theo and perhaps been blissfully happy by now. "What do you want from me?" she asked quietly, almost reverently. She almost feared his answer. No, there was no almost about it. Her fear was palpable and she tasted its bitterness on her tongue.

"I want your happiness," he told her as if the simplicity of that statement could be made true just by voicing it and sending it off into the ether. "Above that I want to spend the rest of my days loving you and ensuring you are not only always protected, but cherished."

Elena looked away. "That's an impossible thing to expect."

"You should expect nothing less." His tone was

fierce, but without reproach. "You should never have been mistreated. I would undo it all if I could. I'd kill him for you, were he not already dead." He closed his eyes. "I wish I had saved you from him."

"None of it was your fault." She shook her head. The blame rested solely on her father. Had he been a better man, she'd never have been forced to marry Dryden. "You have to let me go."

"I don't have to do any such thing." His steadfast gaze told her all she needed to know—Theo wasn't going to walk away. "I love you. I always have, and I'll be damned if I give up easily." He brushed her cheek with his knuckles, a touch so tender it nearly undid her. "It's your decision, darling. It will always be yours, but I am not running away. I'll be here, waiting. And when you're ready, I'll open my arms and welcome you."

She swallowed hard. "Theo..."

"Don't say anything," he said, gently. "Not now. It would be an answer I'm not willing to hear and one you'll regret later. Think on it, and when you're ready to listen to your heart, come find me. I don't make promises lightly and you may trust in me. I will never allow anyone to ever hurt you again." With that, he turned and left her alone.

Theo had given her much to consider. The question was, did she have the courage to open herself to him? Elena wasn't certain she could—even with a man as wonderful as her earl.

Six

Elena didn't know what to think anymore. Her life had been filled with turmoil for so long that she thought she was finally free of all discord. Yet that conversation with Theo had loosened something within her, unraveling the careful control she had over her emotions—if she had ever truly had any. She sucked in a breath, attempting to calm herself, but instead, a tremor began that she could not stop. What was happening to her?

"Are you all right?"

She heard the question and recognized the voice, but her vision was blurred, keeping her from seeing the speaker. Elena turned toward him, shaking her head. She didn't trust her own voice to respond without breaking down. Tears sprang to her eyes, and she furiously wiped them away before they could fall down her cheeks.

"Elena," the man said gently. "Look at me."

She knew him. Of course, she did. She had met all the guests at Lady Winston's house party, but only two men would dare use her given name. One had just left her alone to think about what he'd said. So that left only one possibility. "Eli?" she asked, needing to be sure.

"Yes…" He hurried to her side. "Tell me what's wrong. Let me help."

Eli reached out to pull her close, but she pushed him away. She couldn't allow him to comfort her. "This is all your fault," she accused, her voice harsh. "I wouldn't be in such turmoil if you hadn't arranged for him to be here."

"I don't understand," he said, his voice calm. "What do you mean?"

"You know exactly what I mean. Do not play the fool; it does not suit you." She moved closer, shoving at his chest. "You ensured he would be here. Why are you forcing this upon me? What do you stand to gain?"

Elena knew she sounded like a veritable shrew. The anger spilling forth was beyond her control. It boiled and heated her skin until all she could feel was the depth of that emotion. It consumed her and she allowed it. Because while anger overtook her she could forget about all the other unwanted emotions. The ones that had brought her to the brink of falling apart. At least anger she understood. Anger had gotten her through the years she had been married to a brutish man. Anger had ensured she survived and would continue to do so. Anger felt comfortable like putting on a warm cloak that had always protected her. So she leaned into it and allowed it to rule her in the moment.

"Elena," Eli began, his voice even, as though hoping to calm her. She would not be calmed. Nothing would stop the storm from being unleashed within her. "Listen…"

"To what?" she spat. "Your excuses for shattering the peace I finally found? Because you think you know what is best for me?"

"It is not like that…" Eli held up his hands, perhaps fearing she'd lash out again. "You know I only want your happiness."

"Then you should not have ensured he would be

here." She wanted to smash something, to make a physical statement of her rage. But the conservatory offered nothing for that purpose.

"Who are you speaking of?" he asked, his calm tone only irritating her further.

"You know," she accused. "Stop pretending as if you do not."

"Elena," he started, "I truly do not..."

"Yes, you do," she insisted. "Do not take me for a fool. Did you want to win the wager that badly, hoping he would help you secure a victory?"

"Bloody hell," he cursed. "No wager is worth losing our friendship. I would never do anything to harm you. Please tell me you believe that."

Elena wanted to believe him, but she could not. It could not be mere coincidence that Theo was at this house party. She had kept informed of his movements, if only to brace herself for the inevitable announcement of his marriage to another. But no such announcement had come, and foolishly, hope had blossomed in her heart. Dryden had crushed that hope long ago, warning her that he would never allow her to find happiness if he could not get an heir from her. When he discovered her attachment to Theo, he had beaten her for it and watched her closely, fearing she'd bear a bastard instead of his heir. She had been denied happiness, and though she was grateful Dryden had failed in his efforts to make her a mother, the bitterness lingered.

"He doesn't socialize, Eli." She met his gaze. "The Earl of Northfield is practically a recluse. He attends no social events. He holds meetings, has meals with business associates, but that is all. He doesn't attend Christmastide house parties." She took a step closer. "There would be only one reason for him to attend this one, and it's not the festivities. So tell me, what did you promise him, Eli? What bait did you use?"

He shook his head. "I promised him nothing," Eli sighed. "But you are correct—we do have business dealings, and we have met on such terms." He lifted a hand to cup her cheek. "And yes, he still loves you. But it seems that doesn't matter to you. You're not truly angry with me or him. You're angry with yourself because you're afraid to let anyone close. I'm safe for you because the love we share isn't romantic. We're friends, almost like siblings. But Theo... he makes your heart race. He gives you hope for something you thought you lost years ago." He smiled sadly. "But if hope is too much for you, then that pains me deeply. It means happiness may forever elude you."

"Stop pretending this isn't your fault," she insisted, though she knew, in her heart, that it wasn't.

Elena knew she was unjustly blaming him. Eli had been her friend, the one to help her piece herself back together. He hadn't been the one to hurt her. Instead of arguing further, she turned and walked away, leaving him alone. She could no longer bear this conversation. She needed time to think, to decide what she truly wanted. This argument would not give her the answers she sought.

Theo stood in the library once again. He should have found something to occupy his time earlier, but he had allowed Savorton to distract him. Now he was here, staring at the shelves as if they held all the answers—as if he might uncover some secret that would aid him in his quest to make Elena his once more. He no longer had faith in the outcome he'd hoped for; that hope had disintegrated after their last interaction.

He had told her to think it over and find him when she knew what she wanted. Even as he'd spoken those words, he hadn't truly believed she would come to the conclusion he desired. He should leave the house party. Lady Winston was an excellent hostess, but it was too difficult to remain when the only reason he'd attended no longer wanted him there. The kindest thing he could do for the only woman he had ever loved—would ever love—was to honor her wishes and leave her alone.

"Theo," came Elena's soft voice.

He closed his eyes and took a deep breath, praying he wasn't merely hearing her voice out of desperation. Slowly, he turned and met her gaze. There was a haunted expression in her eyes that made his heart ache. He wished she were not in such turmoil. "Elena," he said reverently. "What may I do for you?"

"I've considered what you said to me earlier." She licked her lips, and he nearly groaned. Oh, how he longed to pull her into his arms and press his lips to hers. That was a desire he feared might never be fulfilled. "And I have made a decision."

Theo braced himself for her answer. He didn't believe for a moment that she wanted to be with him. She was here to let him know, once and for all, and then she would walk away. This time, it would be her choice, and he would have to accept it. He doubted she would ever let go of the shadows that haunted her and allow him to show her true happiness. "And what have you decided, darling?" He could not keep the sadness from his voice; it had been part of him ever since he'd lost her years ago.

She tilted her head to the side and looked up at the ceiling, as if the answer she sought lay hidden there. Then she strolled across the room until she was directly in front of him. "Do you not see it?" she asked.

He narrowed his gaze, puzzled. "I'm afraid I do not."

"Look up, Theo," she insisted.

He glanced toward the ceiling and noticed, for the first time, a sprig of mistletoe hanging directly above them. He hadn't even seen it there before. Why would he? And when had it been hung? More importantly, why did Elena find its presence significant? He turned his attention back to her. "I'm not sure I understand."

She chuckled softly, trailing her fingers over his chest. Heat radiated through him at her touch. Did she wish for him to kiss her? If that was her desire, he would gladly oblige—and he certainly didn't need any mistletoe to do so. He had wanted to kiss her every day for the rest of her life and would not deny himself that pleasure if she offered it. He glanced back up at the mistletoe, then back at her. Was this a blessing he'd never dared hope for? Should he just kiss her and pray for the best? What on earth was he to do?

"Theo, darling," she began, her tone laced with amusement. "I did not think I would have to explain to you what the purpose of mistletoe at Christmastide meant…"

He didn't stop to think. Her words were all the invitation he needed. Theo leaned down, pressing his lips to hers, savoring the feel of her in his arms. He tightened his hold and deepened the kiss. When she opened her mouth on a soft moan, he slipped his tongue inside, tasting her. His desire surged, and he longed to carry her to his room, strip her bare, and explore every inch of her before taking her fully.

Theo tore his mouth from hers before he lost all restraint. His desires, though intense, were secondary to what she needed. He might not know the full extent of her husband's cruelty, but he understood it had left her traumatized. He would do nothing to add to her pain. "I should not have…"

Elena smiled gently, lifting her arms to wrap around his neck as she leaned into him. "Yes, darling, you should have. That's what I came to tell you." She nestled her face into his neck, and he held her close. Theo groaned, overwhelmed by the pleasure of holding her—the pleasure he had convinced himself he would never feel. The warmth of her body against his nearly undid him.

"I don't understand," he managed, his voice unsteady. His breathing was uneven as he fought to maintain control. But she continued to touch him, clouding his thoughts.

"I want you," she said simply. "I want a lover." She lifted her gaze to meet his. "But I do not want a husband." She tilted her head, choosing her next words carefully. "I want to know what it's like to lie with a man and feel pleasure, not pain. Can you do that for me, Theo? Can you spend one night with me —only one night—and show me how it should have been?"

She was offering herself to him—not forever, but for one night. He wanted to refuse because he desired more than a single night with Elena. But would a refusal mean she'd walk away and never look back? Perhaps he should see this as an opportunity—a chance to show her that she wouldn't want to let him go. He nodded slowly. "Yes," he said. "Yes, I will take you to my bed. Tonight, now, and for the entire night. If I only have one night with you, I want it to be all night, to love you completely."

"Then take me to your bed, darling."

He took her hand, leading her from the library. He wouldn't waste another moment, not when he could have her, finally, in his arms.

Seven

Elena followed Theo up to his bedchamber willingly. After considering everything, she had reached one conclusion: her life had been a series of choices made for her, molding her into a woman afraid to take risks. She had become so guarded that it had prevented her from truly living. Once she realized this, she knew what she must do. She might not be able to commit to a future with Theo, but she could have this one night. It would have to be enough, as she could offer him nothing more.

When they reached his bedchamber, Theo pushed the door open and invited her inside. She brushed past him, walking to the center of the room as he moved about, lighting candles that cast a soft glow. It was late enough that no one would expect them for any reason. They had this time, and she was grateful for it. In her internal struggle, she had also discovered something undeniable: she loved Theo. She had always loved him. And while that was no secret, she accepted that, while her love would remain endless, her ability to show him that love would forever be limited. She couldn't give herself freely—not in the way he deserved.

When Theo finished lighting the candles, he returned to her side, leaning down to brush a tender kiss across her cheek. "Are you certain this is what you want?"

The very fact that he asked her made her love him all the more. She adored him for his concern and consideration. If only she could be a different woman… Elena closed her eyes and took a steadying breath. It was time to let go of what could never be. It was better to live in the moment and enjoy what she could. She looked up, meeting his gaze. "Yes," she said. "I want to feel myself in your arms and know that I am the one you desire. I want you to erase everything that haunts me."

"Then that is what we shall do." He brushed a stray lock of her hair behind her ear. "I promise that after tonight, all you will remember is my touch." He leaned close, whispering against her ear, "And when you close your eyes, you'll ache to have me with you again." Then he began to pull the pins from her hair until her auburn locks fell around her shoulder in waves. Theo set the pins down on a nearby table and turned back to her.

A rush of heat surged through her, and her breathing grew ragged. Though they were still fully clothed, his words had seemed to brand her with desire. She ached for him now. Would it always be this way? Would he, indeed, haunt her dreams after this night, leaving her to yearn for him by her side? She shook the thoughts away. If she dwelled on them, she might not be able to enjoy the pleasure that awaited. "Kiss me," she demanded.

"With pleasure, darling." Theo leaned down, pressing his lips to hers, igniting the same instant pleasure and need she'd felt in the library. He pulled away, trailing kisses along her cheek and down to her bosom. He cupped one breast, lowering his mouth to its peak. She gasped as he pushed his hand into her bodice, gently pinching her nipple between his fingers. The slight sting brought far more pleasure than she could have imagined. As he freed her breast and took her aching nipple into his mouth, she moaned.

"You like this, don't you?" he murmured, turning his attention to her other breast, repeating his sensual touches. She writhed in his arms, desperate for more.

"Theo," she breathed his name, her voice husky. "I need…"

"I know, darling," he said. "But first, let's get this gown off. Turn around so I can undo all these tiny buttons. I need to see all of you."

Elena turned, allowing him to work on the buttons. He removed her gown with an expertise she didn't question, though it crossed her mind briefly. She didn't want anything to interrupt this moment. She wanted him more than she had ever wanted anything. Once her gown was gone, he deftly unfastened her corset, leaving her in only her shift and stockings.

"Now," he said, his voice thick with desire. "Take off the shift, darling. Let me see you."

She had never been completely naked before a man before. Yes, she'd been married, but Dryden hadn't made love to her. He shoved up her skirts and took her without preparing her for his invasion. He didn't care about her body. All he had wanted was a child and he didn't need to give her pleasure to achieve that. Slowly, Elena lifted the hem of her shift and lifted it. He sucked in a breath as each part of her naked body was revealed. Then she tore it over her head and let it float to he floor. She still had her stockings and garters on, but for all intents and purposes she was completely naked before him. He stared at her like a man starving and a buffet had just been laid out before him. It was a heady feeling to be the center of such devout concentration.

Theo moved closer, his hands sliding over her belly, then lower to rest on the garters securing her stockings. "I think we'll leave these on for now."

"But..."

"I like them," he said with a wicked smile. "And they won't stop me from loving you."

He lowered his head and kissed her again, making her forget everything else. She had never experienced such pleasure. His hand caressed her hip, then trailed down her stomach. "You're so soft," he murmured. "So beautiful."

Scooping her into his arms, Theo carried her to the bed. She almost protested, fearing the end was near, but he laid her gently on the covers, spreading her thighs as he knelt before her.

"I need to taste you, darling. All of you." He pressed his lips to her inner thigh, then moved to her most sensitive place, kissing her with slow, sensual strokes. She gasped, surrendering to the unfamiliar sensations. He continued, teasing her until she thought she might go mad, then sucked the bundle of nerves at her core. The pleasure overwhelmed her, and her body jolted as waves of ecstasy surged through her, consuming her entirely.

For the first time, Elena understood what it meant to give herself to another, and she knew, despite her fears, this was a moment she would carry with her forever. She'd never felt anything like it and it made her nearly lose consciousness from the sheer pleasure he had given her. It was almost like giving her life over to a higher purpose, but oh, what a way to go.

Theo stared down at Elena's flushed body. Her eyes were closed as she lay languidly upon the bed. He traced his thumb lightly over her skin, studying her unabashedly. This was precisely how he had always imagined her: naked, well-loved, her hair splayed across his bed. He prayed this would not be their only night together, but on the chance it was, he wanted to imprint this sight in his memory forever.

"I know that is not all you do in bed," she

murmured in a husky tone. "You have yet to find your own pleasure."

"My pleasure is incidental," he replied. "This night is for you, to show you how it can be." To convince her that they could have everything if only she would take a chance on him.

"If it is truly for me," she said, a wicked glint in her eye, "then I want you to lose those clothes, darling."

His lips twitched. "I am not sure that is wise. At least, not just yet."

"I insist," she demanded, her tone light but firm. "I refuse to be the only one unclothed." She propped herself on her elbows and studied him. "I want to see all of you. I need to touch you."

Theo closed his eyes and groaned softly. He had promised her an unforgettable night, and it seemed he was prepared to deny her nothing—not even himself. Standing, he began to remove his clothing, starting with his jacket, then his waistcoat, discarding them on the floor without a care. He pulled at his cravat and tossed it onto the bed, an idea sparking in his mind. Something he'd never considered before, yet tonight, a night devoted to her, it seemed fitting. After slipping off his boots and lowering his breeches, he stood naked before her, allowing her to drink in the sight.

"You're beautiful," she whispered.

"You wished to touch me." He swallowed the lump in his throat. "I have a suggestion."

She raised a brow. "You wish to dictate how I touch you?"

"Not at all." He grinned. "However you touch me will bring pleasure beyond my wildest imagination. It is merely a suggestion to allow you control over what happens between us."

"I am listening," she replied, her gaze riveted upon him, though she made no move to close the distance.

He knew this was precisely what she needed. Pleasure, yes, but also control—something to ease the last of her fears. Gesturing to his cravat lying on the bed, he said, "Tie my hands to the headboard. There's a place in the center where you can loop it through and secure each end to my wrists."

Her breath hitched. "But..."

"I will be at your mercy. You know enough to use me as you wish." He grinned, voice low. "And, as I said, any way you touch me will bring me pleasure."

She looked at the headboard, then back at him,

before taking a steadying breath and nodding. "Very well. Come up onto the bed."

He climbed onto the bed and stretched out before her. Following his instruction, she retrieved his cravat and secured him to the headboard. His arousal hardened further as she straddled him, her gaze sweeping over his form, her touch feather-light upon his chest. He inhaled sharply as her fingers grazed his skin. "Yes," he said, his voice rough. "Do that again."

Elena smiled. "Perhaps I will. But not yet." She focused her attention lower, her gaze settling on him as she licked her lips. He groaned, fervently hoping she intended to do as he dreamed. Her fingers slid down his stomach, a teasing trail, until she reached his arousal and traced a single finger along its length. He tensed beneath her touch.

"Elena," he murmured hoarsely. "I need…" He barely restrained himself.

"Soon enough, darling," she replied. "I want to taste you as you did me." Before he could respond, she leaned down, her warm mouth pressing against him as her tongue traced along his cock. He jerked, a low moan escaping his lips as pleasure surged through him. "Oh yes, you enjoy that, don't you?" she murmured, taking him in hand, her palm sliding over him. He hardened further, a feat he had not thought possible.

"I enjoy everything," he assured her.

"Good," she said with a mischievous smile. "Because I am not finished." Leaning down, she took the tip of him into her mouth, and he felt his self-control slipping. The warm, wet heat of her mouth undid him entirely.

"Elena, darling," he said through gritted teeth, "if you continue, I'll spend in your mouth." He was perilously close to doing just that.

"What if that's exactly what I want?" she asked, her gaze playful.

"Then I won't argue." He managed a smile, though his breath was ragged. "But if my wishes mean anything to you, then please…take me inside you. I want you so much."

She paused, tapping her chin thoughtfully before smiling. "As you wish, darling," she said, positioning herself over him.

He held his breath as she lowered herself, guiding him to her entrance. Slowly, she took him in, her body enveloping him in a warmth that made every other experience pale in comparison. She was wet, tight, and utterly his. Perhaps it was more accurate to say he was utterly hers.

Elena began to move, finding her rhythm as he lay bound beneath her. Her beautiful form arched above him, her soft gasps filling the room as she sought her own pleasure. Her inner muscles tightened around him, sending him spiraling closer to his release. As he felt the culmination of their passion build, he gripped the cloth binding his wrists, surrendering to the sensations as he reached his peak. Stars exploded behind his eyes, his release intermingling with her own cries of ecstasy.

This night, this moment, was beyond anything he had thought possible. Their first time together had been everything he had dreamed—and more. It was perfect, because it was with her. He loved her beyond measure, and he prayed, after the night was through she would not be able to walk away from him so easily.

Eight

Sunlight peeked through the drapes in Theo's bedchamber. He hadn't remembered to fully close them when they'd come back to his room the previous night. Elena lay nestled against him, her glorious red hair spilling over his chest, and a surge of happiness spread through him. Stroking the soft locks with reverence, he thought how he would give anything to wake each morning to this sight. She was so utterly lovely that it stole his breath. He adored her and wished to cherish her for the rest of their days. Somehow, he had to make her see how good it could be for them—how they deserved more than just one night.

"Darling," he whispered. "Elena, wake up, love."

She yawned, rolled onto her back, then sat up abruptly. "I'm still in your bed."

"Indeed," he said, smiling. "Come back here and let me kiss you properly."

She shook her head and moved to the edge of the bed, searching for her clothes. Finding her shift, she slipped it over her head, her expression shifting to one of panic as she gathered her gown, stays, and shoes. She still wore her stockings, which had been deliciously distracting the entire night. He frowned and slid out of bed, unbothered by his own nakedness.

"I cannot stay," she said, her voice tense. "The scandal..."

"Elena," he called her name again, hoping to capture her attention. "There's no need to rush off."

"Of course there is." She frowned at him. "The night is over. I should have left before dawn. Surely, someone will see me leaving your bedchamber."

Theo's heart sank. She was truly ending this. He had not believed she could leave him so easily, yet he realized he had been a fool to think otherwise. Clearly, she could not allow herself happiness. That bloody bastard of a husband she'd had ruined her. He sighed, sitting on the bed. Fighting the inevitable would change nothing. Theo had agreed to one night, and he would not insist on more. He loved her, and he would have to let her go. Somehow, he would find a way to live without her. He was not sure how he would accomplish that impossible feat, but he would. Otherwise, what purpose was there in living?

"All right," he said quietly. "Go on, then, and do what you do best. Run away, darling, and retreat to your solitude."

"There is no need to be bitter," she replied, her tone disapproving. "You agreed…"

"I know what I agreed to," he cut in, harsher than he intended. "And I am honoring it. I am not asking you to stay, even though every part of me is begging to do just that. I am watching you walk away from me—for the last time."

"But…" She frowned, confused. "I don't understand."

"I am done, Elena." He scrubbed a hand over his face. "My love for you is not enough, and I can't keep trying. Not that I did much before this house party. Foolishly, I thought you would come to me when you were ready. When it became clear you would not, I came to you." He shook his head, disappointment thick in his voice. "You do not want me—not really. If you did, it would not be so easy to toss me aside as if I meant nothing. It is time I accept that we have no future. You have received what you wanted, darling. I gave you your one night of passion. Go now and protect your reputation."

"Theo," she began. Her eyes were filled with concern but he could not allow himself to stray from the course.

"I do not wish to hear apologies or explanations." He kept his gaze averted. His heart was truly broken. He had lost all hope. Their one night together had been filled with passion, and he would cherish it forever, but nothing could compare to the pain of letting her go. "Do not fret, love. Once you are gone, I will not linger here. I will have my carriage brought around, and you will never have to see me again."

"You do not have to leave," she protested. "Why are you acting this way?"

Slowly, he lifted his gaze to meet hers. The despair he felt must have been evident, spilling from his eyes. "I can't be near you anymore. Don't you understand? It is too difficult for me. I have to go. If I have any chance of moving past what I feel for you, I need distance. I just..." He closed his eyes and swallowed hard. When he opened them, he finished with difficulty. "I just can't."

Elena inhaled sharply. "Theo." She placed a hand over her heart. "I never meant..."

"Darling," he interrupted softly. "There is no need to say anything. I knew what you were asking of me, and it is my burden to bear. I knew you wanted nothing beyond last night. I have no regrets. I would not change a thing. I love you. I adored our time together, and I foolishly hoped you would want more than one night. But you have done nothing wrong. You never promised me anything. Go to your room, love. I will be all right, I promise."

He prayed he could keep that promise, though he doubted he could. It would take time, but he hoped he could live up to his words. She clutched her gown to her chest, then nodded. "Very well. I will leave now, but please...do not depart without saying goodbye."

He could not agree to that. If he saw her again, he might not leave at all. "You best go now, before it is too late to avoid another guest. You still have a chance of escaping this room unnoticed."

She frowned, hesitated, but then turned and left his bedchamber. Once she was gone, he began packing, dressing quickly. He was thankful he did not require a valet; it would make his departure easier, quieter.

With a final glance at the bed where they had shared their night, Theo finished preparing to leave, knowing he was leaving his heart behind.

Several days later...

Elena browsed the shelves of the library. She didn't truly want anything to read, but ever since Theo had left without saying goodbye, she'd been restless. She had hoped a book might soothe her nerves, though none of the volumes on the shelves seemed to hold any appeal.

At the sound of her dearest friend's voice, she tensed. Eli was bound to be less than pleased with her, especially given her recent choices. "Not sure what you wish to read?" he asked.

Turning, she managed a smile, though she didn't feel it. It was merely a pretense—an attempt to feign contentment with the choices she'd made. "I fear I'm experiencing a touch of ennui," she replied, her voice bright yet brittle. "I'm surprised to see you back so soon. I trust your trip was successful?"

"It was," he confirmed, though he offered no details. Leaning against the wall, he crossed his arms. "Do you know where I went?"

Her lips twitched. "I was told you went to procure a special license in time for a Christmas wedding." She moved a little closer. "Was I correctly informed?"

"And if you were?" He arched a brow.

"Then I would say I won our wager." She wiggled her eyebrows playfully, genuinely pleased for him. She had hoped Eli would find happiness. If anyone deserved it, it was him. "And you owe me a boon."

"Perhaps," he conceded with a shrug. "Yet I feel as if I'm the true victor of our little wager." He pushed away from the wall. "I have Gabriella, and she's worth more than any boon you might request from me. Love isn't something to be avoided, Elena. I know you feel something for a certain earl."

She looked away. "I admit to no such thing," she said, unable to meet his gaze. "I'm never marrying again, and love is not an emotion I care to claim."

"You don't love me?" he asked softly. "Is that

why you felt comfortable locking me in a room with Gabriella? Do I mean so little to you?"

Her gaze snapped to his. "That's not the same at all. You mean everything to me. I did that only so you'd finally admit how you feel about her. It was clear you loved her, and yet you resisted." She had no regrets; she had locked him in with Gabriella before going to Theo that night, knowing Eli would eventually confess his heart. Gabriella and Eli belonged together—it was as simple as that.

"I could say the same about you," he replied, his voice gentle. "You're fighting your own feelings." He sighed and shook his head. "But I won't push you. Perhaps one day, you'll allow yourself to love him, or perhaps you'll choose to remain alone and guarded. I cannot force you to seek happiness." He leaned forward and pressed a kiss to her cheek. "Thank you for caring about me, Elena. Now, if you'll pardon me, I have a lady to see about a wedding. You're welcome to attend the ceremony, should you wish to."

He left her standing alone in the library, his words striking her heart like an anvil. He hadn't said anything she hadn't already considered herself. She had made a mistake. She should never have let Theo go.

Suddenly, she knew precisely what she needed to do. Theo had said his farewells and departed, but surely he hadn't meant it. If she went to him, he would welcome her back. Elena closed her eyes, steadying her breath. She could no longer allow her fears to rule her. She had to take a leap of faith and trust in Theo. He had never given her any reason to doubt him. She believed he loved her, and now she needed only to find him and beg his forgiveness.

Theo sat in his study, attempting to focus on his account books, yet he couldn't seem to concentrate. His vision blurred as he looked over the columns of numbers, and he knew it was a futile effort. All he could think about was Elena—and the devastating realization that he had lost her forever. He would never again hold her in his arms.

How had it come to this? He had thought, foolishly perhaps, that enough time had passed since her dreadful husband's death. That now, at last, he might have a place in her life. But he had been utterly wrong in that assumption.

Still, he had no regrets about the night they'd shared. How could he? That night would remain forever cherished in his heart, a memory he could revisit even if he never saw her again.

"My lord," his butler interrupted. "Pardon the intrusion."

"What is it, Bivens?" Theo asked, glancing up.

"There's a caller..."

Theo frowned. He wasn't expecting visitors, especially during the Christmastide season when most people were with family. "Did they leave a card?"

"No, my lord," Bivens replied, a hint of hesitation in his voice. "It's...well, there is no delicate way to say this. It is a woman."

Theo stood abruptly. He knew who he hoped had come to his door, but he dared not give in to such dangerous optimism. If he allowed himself to believe that Elena was here, in his home, he might truly lose his mind if it turned out otherwise. Swallowing, he closed his eyes briefly, bracing himself. "Bring her here," he said, steeling himself for disappointment.

He moved to the window, looking out over the frozen, dormant garden awaiting the first bloom of spring. At the start of Lady Winston's house party, he'd had high hopes for a joyous Christmastide only to watch them crumble. He'd risked his heart for Elena's love, and lost. Now he was left, a wretched man, resigned to the life that stretched out before him, empty and bleak.

"Theo," a soft voice said behind him.

It was her voice. Yet surely, he was imagining it. He remained motionless, his heart pounding. He feared turning around, afraid to face either the joy or the despair her presence might bring. Slowly, he turned to see her standing there. She was as beautiful as he remembered, her cheeks flushed from the cold.

"Elena," he breathed, scarcely believing his eyes. "Why are you here?"

She crossed the room, standing before him. "I made a mistake."

"Did you?" He raised a brow, uncertain, holding himself back. "And what mistake would that be?"

"I should never have asked for only one night with you."

He sighed. "I already told you—"

"Let me finish," she said softly, her gaze earnest. "I should have demanded much more than that. One night was not enough. Not for us." She reached up to cup his cheek. "A lifetime wouldn't be enough. I love you, my dearest, and I owe you an apology. I know you didn't ask for one, but you deserve it. I used you for my own selfish purposes, and you allowed it because you're a good man, wanting only to treat me as something precious."

"You are everything to me," he replied quietly. "No one else could mean more."

"I know," she said, her voice trembling. "Please forgive me, love. Tell me it isn't too late, and that you still want me."

Theo closed his eyes, taking in a steadying breath. He prayed this wasn't some fevered dream. If it were, he wouldn't survive the reality. "My darling," he murmured, his tone soft, welcoming. "I love you beyond measure. I want forever with you. Always. We don't have to marry if that is your concern. I only want you near, for the rest of my days."

She smiled, her eyes shimmering with emotion. "I adore you for offering me that, but I do wish to marry. I want more than forever—I want the promise of eternity. I never want to be parted from you again."

"Thank heaven," he whispered. He pulled her into his arms, his lips finding hers in a kiss that was both a reunion and a vow. It was a promise, an edict, and everything in between. Theo could not love her more than he did in that moment, with her standing there, having braved her fears to come back to him. As if he could have ever denied her... He could hardly wait to begin their lives together, to marry her and start the future they'd long been denied.

He would have waited forever for her, but thankfully, he didn't have to. She held his heart—and he prayed she would never let go, just as he would never let go of her.

Epilogue

Five years later...

Elena walked slowly to the parlor, her belly rounded with the child she carried. This would be her third child with Theo. Her first marriage had brought her no children, but it was now clear the fault had not been hers. Shortly after marrying Theo, she had discovered she was with child—their first night together had resulted in that happy surprise. Eight months later, they had welcomed their daughter, a beautiful girl with Elena's auburn hair and her father's brilliant blue eyes. Olivia was now four years old, and her little brother, Elijah, had turned two the previous month. She and Theo had named him in honor of her dear friend Elias. If not for his actions she may never have found her way back to Theo. For that she would forever be grateful to him.

The new baby was due in a few months, but already she felt an ache in her back. She found Theo in the parlor with their two little darlings.

"Daddy," Olivia was saying, "tell me the story again."

He grinned down at her cherubic face. "Haven't you heard it enough, my love?"

"No," she replied, sticking her thumb in her mouth. "Tell it!"

Elijah clapped his hands as if he understood everything. He was a darling little boy, the very image of his father. Elena smiled as she watched her little family. She never would have had this joy if she had let her fears control her. Now, she couldn't imagine life any other way.

"All right," Theo said, settling in. "Once upon a time, in an enchanted world, lived an evil king, along with a princess so pure and beautiful she stole the hearts of all who sought her hand."

Elena grinned. Was it any wonder their daughter adored this tale? Theo was a master storyteller, even if he embellished a little.

"But her heart belonged to just one man," he

continued. "The evil king tried to keep her away from her love, and for a time, he succeeded. The princess faced many trials before she could be with her true love." His gaze lifted to meet Elena's. "But her love waited for her, for he could not imagine life without her. And when the time was right, they overcame every obstacle. Through magic and faith, they were finally able to be together."

"And they lived happily ever after?" Olivia asked, her eyes wide.

"The happiest," Theo assured her, still looking at Elena. "Now, I think it's time for you two to go to the nursery. It's time for your nap."

"I don't want to take a nap," Olivia pouted.

"Me neither," Elijah echoed.

"Well, I want a nap," Theo said a mischievous grin spread across his handsome face. "And so does Mommy."

The children squealed with delight and ran over to hug her. "Do you want a nap, Mommy?" Olivia asked.

Elena rubbed her belly, smiled down at them, and then met Theo's heated gaze. Oh, the rogue—he didn't want a nap at all. He wanted to strip her bare and have his wicked way with her. Heat simmered in her as she realized how much he still desired her after all these years. She was ever so fortunate to have his love. "I *am* very tired," she told her children. "A good rest would do us all well, don't you think?"

"Fine," Olivia said, reluctantly. "I will take a nap, but only so you can rest too, Mommy."

Elena kissed her daughter. "Thank you, my love. I do appreciate your kindness." She hugged them both. "Now, off you go to the nursery. Nanny is waiting."

They grumbled but trotted off as they were told. Once alone, Theo came to her side, pulling her into his arms. "Have I told you how much I love you?" he murmured.

"Only every day, several times a day, for the past five years," she teased, smiling up at him. "And I adore you too, husband."

"Let's go take that nap." He winked. "I have a mind to show you just how much I adore you."

Elena laughed, happiness brimming over. To think she had nearly walked away from him—what a fool she would have been. "Lead the way," she said, slipping her hand into his. "An afternoon nap sounds delightful. What wicked fun we shall have…"

Thank you so much for taking the time to read my book.
Your opinion matters!
Please take a moment to review this book on your favorite review site and share your opinion with fellow readers.

www.authordawnbrower.com

Excerpt: Her Duke to Savor

WAYWARD DUKES' ALLIANCE

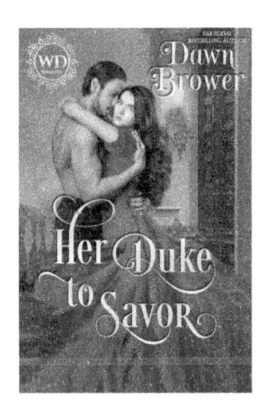

Blurb

Elias Stevens, the Marquess of Savorton doesn't believe he'll ever fall in love. He may marry one day, because the title demands it; however, that elusive emotion will not be freely given to his future wife.

A house party changes everything for him though. His dearest friend makes a wager with him. He'll fall in love by the new year. Elias takes that bet because he knows his own heart.

Lady Gabriella St. Giles lives a charmed life. She has a good family and fully believes one day she'll meet a gentleman sure to steal her heart. What she doesn't count on is meeting an scandalously intriguing marquess at a house party.

Love is on the agenda. One of them wants it and the other hopes to desperately escape it. That wager gives the marquess far more than he could ever imagined, and Gabriella may just acquire her own future duke to savor.

Prologue

Elias Stevens, the Marquess of Savorton, leaned in his chair and then rocked it on the back two legs as he studied his cards. How many should he discard? After pondering it for a few moments, he set his chair back down on all four legs and leaned on the table. He plucked five cards out of his hand and placed them face down on the table, and then drew five more from the deck carefully arranging them with the ones he still held.

He refrained from grinning at the cards he'd added to his hand. He glanced up at his dearest friend, Elena, the Dowager Countess of Dryden. Her dark red hair shimmered in the candlelight, and there was a gleam in her light gray eyes. She was studying her own cards. The two of them were engrossed in a duel of sorts as they played a grueling game of piquet. This was their last hand in a set of six and would determine which one of them came out the winner. It was a close game and either of them might be declared the victor.

"It's your turn, love," Eli reminded her and tapped a finger impatiently on the table.

"I'm aware," she drawled. "I do not need your guidance." Elena winked. "I'm a far better player than you are."

"Debatable," he replied in an arrogant tone. "I am not so certain you're correct."

Her lips lifted into one of her sensual smiles. It was the type of smile that would set most men aflame with desire, but Eli felt nothing. For him that smile meant something far different. The minx was about to pounce and he would end up metaphorically wounded after she made her strike. Hell. She was going to win, and he didn't like it.

"You always did hate losing," she replied in a glib tone. She removed three cards from her hand and then replaced them with three more from the deck. "There's no need for deliberations. We both know the truth."

"That piquet is a game of chance?" Eli lifted a

brow. "In that you are correct." He refused to admit defeat until he absolutely had to.

She laughed and then grinned at him. "I suppose that is true with any game used for the purpose of gambling. Luck may or may not be on your side." She rearranged her cards in her hand. "But we both know piquet is much more than that. It requires skill, strategy, and an excellent memory. I happen to have all three."

Eli shook his head and sighed and made his declarations, and they continued on with the game. After they were done playing, he had to confess, "I concede, you won." He met her gaze. "I'm not saying you are a better player though."

"Of course you will not. I'd expect nothing less." Her gray eyes sparkled with mischief. "You never have. Why would you change that core part of you now?"

They were at Elena's London townhouse. Many members of the ton believed they were lovers, but nothing could be farther from the truth. Elena and Eli had been friends since they were children. He was only three years older than her, and they first met when he was four and she could barely stand to walk in the nursery. Their mothers had been close and that had brought them together often. Eli was as protective of Elena as he would be if he'd had a sister. When she had married an old man, he had tried to persuade her against the match, but she reminded him they all had their duties to perform and her marriage landed firmly in that column. Her father had arranged the marriage, and she had done as she was told.

Elena had regretted it as her marriage made her miserable. Her husband hadn't been abusive, exactly, but he'd been cold. When she failed to conceive, he'd treated her as if she were a useless person. He may never have physically hit her, but his words were like blows that failed to leave a visible bruise. Eli had never been happier when the earl ceased breathing. When the Earl of Dryden dropped dead suddenly Eli had rejoiced, and secretly so had Elena.

"Do you think you'll ever remarry?" he asked in a noncommittal tone.

She snorted. "Not bloody likely. One marriage of inconvenience is enough to turn me away from such an endeavor." Elena gathered the cards and stacked them neatly on the table. "Why do you ask?"

He didn't want to tell her he'd been thinking about how unhappy she had been. Elena enjoyed being a widow. She had freedom and if she wanted a lover, she could and probably had taken one. Not that, to his knowledge, she did… Eli didn't ask her about anything he didn't really want answers to. "What if you fell in love?"

"That is even more unlikely. Love is a myth they try to make a woman believe." She leaned back and studied him. "Are you in love, Eli?"

"Absolutely not," he said in an emphatic tone. "Unless you count that gorgeous opera singer, I spent an evening with a few nights ago. She was delicious and might convince me I could believe in love."

He was far too busy helping build Savorton Shipping. His family had struggled when he was younger and now that he could, he worked to make their fortune something that rivaled even the most affluent in English society. He was an heir to a dukedom and now the estate thrived. His father had become frail in his old age and left running all the estates to Eli, but still offered input when he felt it was required. Eli did not have time for love.

"A night of passion is not love," Elena replied in a dry tone. "Neither of us is on the market for that elusive emotion."

"So you do not believe you will ever willingly give your heart away?" This seemed like an opportunity. Should he take it? Elena had never really given any man a chance, and she had good reason for that. As a widow of wealthy means, she didn't have to remarry, but she had a past she seemed determined to forget. One he wanted to remind her about in a subtle way. "You don't have to marry a man if you love him, you know."

"I'm aware," she said, then tilted her head to the side. "I never have to marry again. But you do."

"I've never been married, love," he replied. "I cannot marry again when I never have."

"You are purposely misunderstanding me," she accused. "You know perfectly well what I meant. You're going to be a duke one day and you need heirs."

"I was hoping to convince you to marry me," he said in a smooth tone. "You're the only woman I actually like."

"What a vile thing to suggest." She glared at him. "The very idea of sharing a bed with you..." Elena shuddered.

"Now that wasn't necessary. I'm not revolting." He frowned. She made a valid argument, though. Eli didn't wish to bed her any more than she wanted to join him in that activity.

"Darling," she began as she studied him. "You

are passably handsome. I've heard many debutantes expound on your breathtaking visage. Apparently, your black hair and green eyes make them swoon with desire."

"Of course, they do. What they actually desire to be a future duchess, and my gorgeous physique has nothing to do with their admiration." Eli might be a bit jaded... "I am not marrying until I absolutely have to, and love won't be part of the bargain."

"That's too bad," she said in a somber tone. "You're destined to have a marriage like mine."

"I won't be a brute like your husband was. I'd never treat a woman so callously." He wouldn't. Eli had to believe he'd be better than the late Earl of Dryden. Elena was still young and only eight and twenty. She could find someone to be happy with. Somehow, he had to convince her to try.

"Perhaps not," she agreed. "You might be the one that is emotionally abused. I pray you choose wisely."

"I'll have you approve of my future wife." He smiled. "You may have better judgement than me."

"I already do," she said, then laughed. "Perhaps we should make a wager."

It couldn't be that easy... She was playing right

into his plans. Elena was a lot like him. She hated to lose. "What sort of wager?"

She tapped on the cards. "All gambling is a matter of chance, but some games are a little more than that. Much like piquet, love can be played in a similar fashion."

"So we use our strategy and skill to avoid falling?" he asked, trying to understand her meaning.

"In a sense," she replied. "We will also have to keep track of all the players, for unlike our little game here, there will be more than two."

"And what exactly is this wager?" Eli asked.

"How about we make it simple," she began. "The first to fall in love by the end of Christmastide loses and owes the other a boon."

He pondered her suggestion. "And what if neither of us falls?"

"Then we both win," she said in a wistful tone. "Or perhaps we will both lose, depending on one's perspective."

Eli doubted he would fall in love. He had yet to meet a woman that inspired such an insipid emotion in him. "All right, I accept. In fact, I have the perfect playing field for us."

She lifted a brow. "Oh?"

"Lady Winston is having a house party. It begins

EXCERPT: HER DUKE TO SAVOR

in a couple of weeks and will extend through the entirety of Christmastide. My mother has been hounding me to attend. I'll tell her I will as long as you go and we can put our wager to the test."

Elena steepled her fingers together. "Excellent," she said in a gleeful tone. "Let the best player win, then."

He was going to enjoy watching her fall, for he knew something she did not. The Earl of Northfield would be in attendance. Elena had never said as much, but the earl had been her first and only love. One she had never had a chance at having a relationship with. Elena had shoved those feelings deep inside her and prepared to marry the Earl of Dryden as her father had ordered. Perhaps this was her second chance at finding happiness.

He wasn't worried about himself. Eli had time to find a suitable wife. His concern was for his dearest friend and helping her find a love she deserved. Besides he hadn't lied, Eli didn't believe in love, at least not when it came to his own life. Love was for other people. Individuals who had the luxury of accepting that gift into their lives. Eli would never be that fortunate.

One

Lady Gabriella St. Giles sat at her vanity and slid a brush through her long black locks until they were shiny and smooth. Now all she had to do was plait in and wrap it up into a knot above her neck. She could have her maid, Ruth, fix her hair, but she liked to be independent when she could manage it. This was one thing she could do for herself. Besides, she didn't need anything fancy for a dinner at home with her parents. Her brother and sister were not even going to be in attendance. All that was left at home was her. Both of her siblings had married, and that left her all by herself.

Her parents loved her. She didn't doubt that, but she couldn't talk to them. Not like she could with her sister. Her closest friend, Clara Adams, understood that loss too. When Clara's father died, she had gone with her mother to live at her grandfather's estate. Her grandfather was the Viscount of Redcliffe. Clara's sister, Juliet, had a different mother and hadn't been so fortunate. She'd had to take work as a lady's companion to survive. Clara hadn't spoken to her sister since their father died, but she'd heard the rumors. Juliet would marry the notorious Duke of Sin soon and she would become the Duchess of Sinbrough. Clara had admitted she'd been envious of her sister, but she missed her more. Even though Juliet would be a duchess, Mrs. Adams still refused to allow Clara to visit her sister. The Duke of Sinbrough's reputation made him unimpressive in Mrs. Adams estimation even with his lofty title.

Gabriella understood that. She missed her own sister, Genevieve, too, but she was now the Duchess of Argyle and had her own household to run. It was kind of ironic that both Clara's sister and Gabriella's had married a duke. That was just another thing they had in common.

She finished plaiting her hair and wound it into a knot, then secured it with hairpins. Satisfied with her ministrations, she stood and smoothed down her skirts. Gabriella was on a mission. After her visit

EXCERPT: HER DUKE TO SAVOR

with Clara earlier that day, she knew how she wanted to spend the Christmastide season. Lady Winston was having a house party, and she wanted to attend. Clara was already set to travel with her mother, Mrs. Adams, and invited her to attend with them.

Gabriella's mother hated house parties, especially during the colder months. Mainly because she hated to travel. Not that she blamed her mother. As the Marchioness of Hollibrook, she shouldn't be required to do anything she didn't wish to do. But that didn't mean that she should suffer because of it. Surely, her mother would understand why she wished to travel to Lady Winston's home for the holiday season. Gabriella wanted to have a little fun and maybe try to find her own happiness.

She left her room and went in search of her mother. She found the marchioness in her favorite sitting room working on her needlepoint. Her mother slid her needle into the fabric and created a cross stitch that was both elegant and intricate in design. "Who is that for?" Gabriella asked.

"I'm not certain yet." The marchioness glanced up and smiled at Gabriella. "One of my children should make me a grandmother soon, I would think. This will be for whatever baby is born first."

Gabriella lifted a brow. "You have high expectations, don't you? What if Genevieve or Everett decide to wait to bring a child into the world? Then what will you do with that piece of art?"

Her mother shrugged elegantly, like she did all things. "It'll hold until it is needed. It's not as if it'll spoil while it waits for the intended recipient to be born."

"That is true," Gabriella said, then sat on the chair next to where her mother worked on her needlepoint. "Mother," she began. "I wish to discuss Christmastide with you."

Her mother glanced at her and lifted her brow. "Is that so?" She set the loom on a nearby table. "Go on. What is it you wish to discuss?"

Gabriella now had her mother's full attention. She wasn't certain that was an entirely good outcome. It might have been better if her mother had remained distracted as Gabriella spoke. "I've been invited to attend Lady Winston's house party with Miss Clara Adams and her mother."

The marchioness frowned. "I would rather you stay here with your family." She tapped her finger on the arm of her chair. "And I don't care for Mrs. Adams. I attended finishing school with her and she's always been..." She stopped as if searching for the right word. "I suppose that doesn't bear repeating. Suffice to say she's not a pleasant woman."

"I cannot disagree with you on that score," Gabriella told her mother. "In my opinion, you're offering a kindness where one isn't deserved. She's perfectly horrid to Clara." And what kind of woman throws her stepdaughter on the streets with nothing to aid her? When she had learned what Millicent Adams had done to Juliet, she'd cringed, and poor Clara was stuck in the middle of it all. "However, I would still like to attend with them. Clara needs a friend when all she has is her mother to lean on."

Her mother was silent for several seconds. "As much as I hate to admit this... I agree with you." She slumped a little in her chair. Her mother never slumped. This couldn't be good... "Clara needs a friend like you. I'll allow you to go, but I'm not happy about this situation. I would much rather go with you, but your father's been ill, and I don't wish to leave him."

"I didn't think his illness was serious." Alarm spiked through her at her mother's concern.

"It isn't," her mother said. "But that doesn't mean he should travel and make it worse. I'll stay with him, and I'm going to trust you to act like a lady of your station. If a scandal of some sort arises out of this house party, your name best not be attached to it."

Gabriella's lips twitched as she fought a smile. "I promise not to elope to Scotland with the first rake that crosses my path. However, shall I resist..." She lifted her arm on to her forehead in a woe is me pose.

"There's no need to be cheeky with me," she said, but she smiled. "You know how you're to present yourself. Be the lady you were raised to be."

"I will, mother," she promised. "Now I'm going to summon Ruth so she can pack my trunks, and I need to send a missive to Clara to inform her that I will be joining them."

"I'll miss you when you are gone," her mother said. "I hope it will be a pleasant excursion."

"Me too," Gabriella said, then left her mother alone to do her needlepoint. She had a lot to do before her upcoming trip to the English countryside.

The carriage rolled across the road as smooth as one could on a road with the occasional hole in it. When a wheel bounced over one of those holes, it would toss Gabriella into the side with a hard thump. She was starting to regret her choice to travel with Clara and her mother to Lady Winston's house party. Not because of the rough roads and frigid weather. That she could endure if needed. No, her issue had nothing to do with anything so mundane.

"Clara don't slouch. Ladies do not slouch." Mrs. Adams glared at her daughter.

Gabriella barely refrained from rolling her eyes. They were in a carriage on a long journey. Slouching was a necessity at times. How could Mrs. Adams expect her daughter to remain stiff and unmoving? Especially when they were bouncing around the carriage whenever they hit an unfortunate bump?

"I'm trying, mother," Clara said in a frustrated tone. "It's not as easy as you seem to believe."

"You're not trying hard enough," Mrs. Adams chastised her. "I'm not having the same difficulty you are."

Gabriella mashed her teeth together. How could a woman as rotten as Mrs. Adams be the mother of a girl as sweet as Clara? If she could have intervened, she would have, but it wasn't her place. She was their guest for this excursion, and she had to be as polite as possible. "We should arrive at Lady Winston's soon," she told Clara. "Then you will be free from this carriage." Unfortunately, Clara would never be free from her mother's disapproval.

"And when we get there, you best act like the lady I raised you to be," Mrs. Adams said. "You're the granddaughter of a viscount. Do not shame our family and act like a hellion."

"I promise I will do nothing you don't approve of," Clara said in a meek tone. That poor girl...

The carriage turned, and they were finally going down the long drive to Winston Manor. Lady Winston was a widow and quite wealthy in her own right. Her son was a mere ten years old and the new Earl of Winston. Somehow, Lady Winston had convinced her husband that she should remain in control of her son's inheritance. Which meant she remained at Winston Manor as long as her son was a child. When he was older and ready to start a family of his own, she would most likely remain in London at the townhouse she owned separately from the Winston estate. The widow had always fascinated Gabriella, and she conversed with her when she could. She liked the idea of having control over her own fate and often thought that perhaps marriage was not something she wanted to agree to.

She had a fortune of her own that her father settled on her. Gabriella also had a dowry that was separate from her inheritance. She could live her life without ever marrying if that is what she chose to do, and she might. That decision was not something she wished to make yet. "This estate is gorgeous," Gabriella said as she peered out the window. "In the summer, it must be breathtaking. Even with snow and ice as decoration it is quite imposing to behold."

"Surely it is not as grand as your grandfather's estate," Mrs. Adam said in a shrill tone. "This is the estate of an earl. A duke would have something far more impressive."

Gabriella frowned. "Cranbrook Castle is breathtaking." She wrinkled her nose. "But traveling there is a bit tedious. His estate borders the lowlands of Scotland. He's actually friendly with some of his Scottish neighbors and some of his servants are Scottish."

"You have something against the Scots?" Clara asked.

"Not at all," Gabriella clarified. "It's merely an observation. Traveling that far north is not something we do often. Father's estate is much closer to London if we need to stay in the country. Mother prefers to be in town and father humors her request."

"I like the country better," Mrs. Adams said. "But

my father insists we stay in London. I believe he doesn't enjoy having us near him."

She almost sounded sad... "I'm sorry," Gabriella said. Mostly because she didn't know what else to say. Thankfully, she was saved from having to continue the conversation when the carriage came to a stop. A footman opened the door immediately and helped them out of the carriage.

"Welcome to Winston Manor," a man said from the entrance. "Please come inside. Your trunks will be unloaded and taken to your rooms."

Gabriella smiled at him. "Thank you."

"More guests have arrived." Lady Winston clapped her hands together in glee. "I'm so happy you could join us for Christmastide. You all will want to rest and freshen up. The evening meal is in two hours. I will have a maid show you to your chambers. You can stay there and rest or you may join the other guests in the large salon. I've set up various games and activities in there for your entertainment. Just ask the maid directions if that is what you choose to do." She beamed at them. "Now I have some other tasks to see to. Welcome again." She waved at them and wandered off.

Gabriella would have liked to speak with her more, but she supposed she could later. They were there for the next couple of weeks and there was time for that. She followed the maid up to her assigned chamber and smiled because she had a room to herself. How wonderful! She hadn't expected to be that lucky. She would enjoy the solitude when she needed it.

Order Here: https://books2read.com/Herduketosavor

Excerpt: A Lady Never Tells

LADY BE WICKED BOOK ONE

The first book in an all new series: Lady Be Wicked featuring Eden, The Countess of Moreland from Her Rogue for One Night

Blurb

Eden Barrett, the Countess of Moreland, is a young widow. Her foolish husband died in a duel, after having an affair with her closest friend. With one affair her entire life changed. Having freedom for the first time in her life she embraces it. Roslyn, her sister by marriage, is about to debut and Eden is her chaperone, and she's determined to aid her to find a husband that won't disappoint her.

Maxwell Holden, the Duke of Carrington has decided it is time to find himself a wife. He has a list of requirements and Lady Roslyn Barrett is the perfect candidate. There is only one problem: her chaperone. Something about her is oddly familiar, and he's more drawn to the young widow than he likes. The more time he spends with her, the more he can't stay away.

Eden is determined never to marry again. Especially to the Duke of Carrington. She has a secret though and if he discovers it everything will change. They've met before, and she's determined he never realizes exactly how they're acquainted. Secrets don't stay buried though, and this one is about to come to the light...

Order Here: **https://books2read.com/ALadyNeverTells**

Prologue

Her anxiety had hit an all-new level. Eden Barrett, the Countess of Moreland, did not take risks. It went against her very nature to do so. Yet, that was exactly what she was about to do. She'd willingly accepted an invitation to the Duke of Sinbrough's masquerade ball. It was literally entering into a den of iniquity. Sin itself would be on full display at this ball. The duke was famous for having the most debauched parties for anyone who wished to attend. It was rumored even the most strait-laced ladies would don a mask and join the festivities.

She should be all right. Shouldn't she?

If she kept telling herself that then perhaps, she would be. She'd convinced her good friend, Mrs.

Claudine Grant to attend the masquerade with her. She'd even commissioned scandalous costumes for them both. Eden's gown was the pure white of innocence, but it was anything but that. It was made for sin, and she hoped she would live up to the invitation it presented.

Her mask was also white to match the gown, but it had ruby red feathers fashioned to it on one side. A little splash of color to show she wasn't as innocent as the dress may suggest. Just in case the low-cut bodice didn't do the job. She had left her golden blonde hair loose and flowing down her shoulders. Her mask kept them from going wild, but if it was removed then they might just become unruly.

"Are you ready?" Claudine asked.

"As I'll ever be." She smiled at her. Eden tried to embrace her inner wickedness, but so far it seemed to be hidden. "Someone is about to approach us." She nodded slightly at the direction of two gentlemen making their way through the crowd. "I do believe the gowns are working." She'd had Claudine's gown designed in a decadent pink that nearly matched her friend's skin tone.

Claudine grinned. "One of them is the man I hoped to see tonight. I'd recognize him anywhere."

"How fortunate that he's noticed you as well."

When the two men reached their side Claudine's love interest stared at her briefly before he held out his hand and said, "Dance with me." Claudine went off with him willingly leaving Eden alone with the other gentleman.

"Would you like to take a spin around the floor." The man said.

There was definitely something sinful about him. His hair was as black as his clothing, and his eyes were a very pretty green. She tilted her head to the side and studied him. "You're the Duke of Sin aren't you."

"Was I being too obvious?" He grinned. "Would you like me to live up to that moniker?"

Eden wasn't interested at all in him. He might be sexy as well, sin, but she didn't find him all that interesting. She wanted to feel something. She didn't know exactly what, just that he didn't do anything for her. She shook her head. "No, thank you."

Someone laughed from behind her. "Have you lost your touch old man."

The Duke of Sinbrough frowned. "Don't be ridiculous. That would never happen." He wiggled his eyebrows at Eden as if that said everything. "We're just becoming acquainted."

Eden turned around to glance at the man who had just entered behind her. He didn't wear all black like most of the men in the room. However he had not bothered to wear a waistcoat and jacket. He had on dark blue pantaloons and a stark white shirt, but no cravat. He had left his shirt open giving her a nice view his neck, and part of his chest. The gentleman was completely disheveled. His hair wasn't nearly as dark as the Duke of Sinbrough's. It was more brown than black, but his eyes were a similar shade of green. Where she had found the duke's pretty, this man's were filled with heat.

That heat spread over her like a whirlwind. She'd been looking for someone to spark something in her. Eden had started to believe that she couldn't feel true passion. What was it about this man that made her want more? Was this desire? How had she never felt anything like it before. She took a step toward him and tilted her lips upward into what she hoped was a wanton smile. "Do you think you can do better?"

He returned her smile and it sent shivers right through her. "I know I can," he told her. "Would you like me to try?"

"You mean you haven't already?" She tilted her

head to the side. "Wasn't that what you were doing when you slid your way behind us?"

He chuckled softly. "You may be right." He leaned forward and said in a demanding tone. "I want you?"

"Do you?" She licked her lips. "I might let you have me." She stepped closer and trailed her finger over his collarbone. "But the night is still young. I have many options. What makes you my best choice?"

She'd never flirted like this in her entire life. Eden felt alive for the first time. The thrill of this was beyond even her wildest imagination. He stepped closer until her breasts rubbed against his warm chest. Her nipples tightened at the mere hit of his heat and the pleasure was intoxicating. He leaned down until his mouth was near her ear. His breath caressed her skin making her even hotter with need. "Darling," he said in a husky tone. "You already decided. Don't make me beg."

Her throaty chuckle sounded foreign to her ears. Who was this wicked, wanton, widow allowing this unknown gentleman to seduce her? She didn't recognize herself but wasn't that why she'd come to this masquerade. She slid her hand down and pulled out his shirt from his pantaloons, then slid it underneath until her fingers met his naked flesh. She trailed her fingers up his chest and then around his waist. He yanked her closer. "You're playing with fire, love."

"But what a burn it'll be," she replied in a husky tone. "You did say you wish to play with me tonight. Dazzle me with your skills."

"It'll be my pleasure," he said as he lowered his mouth. When his lips touched hers, she forgot everything, even her own name. Yes. This is what she had come to the masquerade for. She hadn't known what she'd been looking for until he'd come near. Damn this was good, and she suspected as the night rolled on she'd experience more passion than she'd ever known in her marriage.

She wanted him, and she'd have him. Then after this night she would go back to the proper Countess of Moreland. She had to keep up appearances after all. There were people that depended on her. But for this one night she could have him and all the pleasure this kiss promised. No one else had to know. A lady never tells her secrets, and this one she would always hold dear.

Order Here: **https://books2read.com/ALadyNeverTells**

One

A bead of sweat trailed down Eden's forehead. She wanted to wipe the moisture away, but her hands were otherwise occupied. They were, in fact, full of bolts of fabric she desperately wished to place somewhere else. Roslyn, her sister-in-law, was currently being fitted for several more gowns for her debut season. The shopping seemed to be never ending, and all Eden wanted to do was hide away in her sitting room and read. The idea of the upcoming season distressed her. She didn't like the *ton* or society, and had never had a debut season of her own.

"Are you certain you wish to have gowns made from all of this?" Eden lifted the bolts so Roslyn could see them. "You already have..."

"I don't have enough gowns. Do you have any sense of the amount of balls, soirees, and picnics we are about to be invited to?" Roslyn lifted a brow. "More than even I can imagine, and I can picture many." The girl sighed. She was standing in the center of the seamstress's dressing room while the woman frantically pinned her hem in place. "I have been waiting so long for this, and I do not want to be a failure because I lack the necessary attire."

Roslyn had a similar coloring as Eden. They could be mistaken for sisters in truth, and not just by marriage. Though Eden was a head shorter than Roslyn, they both had golden blonde hair. Their eyes were both a light shade, but Roslyn's was blue and Eden's green. "I understand that you feel you're at a disadvantage." Eden didn't get to finish her thought before Roslyn turned her head to glare at her.

"My brother is, was, a fool," she said with enough vehemence to slice a person to ribbons. "His death, while unfortunate, was easily preventable if he'd had the good sense to use the intelligence his birth had given him."

"Some might say that his lack of intelligence is what led to his demise," Eden said drolly. Her marriage had not been a love match. Her father, and the late Lord Moreland's father, had wanted the union. Neither of them had been given a choice. Perhaps, if love had been a part of their marriage, William never would have strayed, and with Eden's dearest friend at that. She'd lost her friend and her husband in one act of selfishness.

Roslyn laughed. "I shouldn't find that funny," she said between chuckles. "But there is too much truth in that statement to ignore its veracity." Roslyn took several deep breaths in an attempt to get her laughter under control. "In all seriousness, most gentlemen don't stop to think about how an amorous affair might lead to disastrous consequences. My brother was more foolish than most. Not only did he tup his best friend's wife, that very wife was your friend too. How did he not realize that was a horrible decision?"

Eden shrugged. "I stopped trying to deduce the inner workings of your brother's mind many months ago." While she'd been grieving the loss of her reputation more than his death. The *ton* spoke about her in hushed tones that were not as hushed as they thought them to be. Eden didn't know if Roslyn realized how much the *ton* gossiped about their family, and that it might make her chances of finding a husband harder than it should be. Even though they were about to enter society and it might be a battle, Eden was determined that Roslyn would not have a husband like William. One of them should find a gentleman who believed in marriage and love. Eden had given up on that for herself. It was enough that she didn't have to worry about how she'd survive and that her young son would always be safe.

"Set that fabric over there," Roslyn gestured with her hand. "I've already discussed with Madam Broussard what type of gowns I would like. She'll know what to do with them." She smiled. "I hope you have had some new gowns made as well."

She had, but not nearly as many as Roslyn had ordered. "I won't embarrass you."

"You never would." Roslyn's smile faded. "You're too young to be alone. You should reconsider your decision to never remarry."

Roslyn was only four years younger than her. Eden had turned three and twenty a couple months earlier, and she couldn't imagine ever trusting another man with her life again. She was finally free from the dictates of a man, and she had some trusted friends, widows like herself, she could rely on. Eden didn't need to remarry. "I am content with my life."

"But we're finally out of mourning…"

"And that's a good thing. It allows you to have your debut now. It is enough that you wish to marry, and we will ensure you have a good husband." One that wouldn't be unfaithful and hold her in the highest regard. "I'm happy with my circumstances." She smiled as brightly as she could, even though she didn't feel particularly happy at that moment. Eden was hot and irritable. All she wanted to do was go home and rest. It had been a trying day. "Don't distress yourself unnecessarily. I promise I'll be all right once you marry and move away."

Roslyn stared at her for several moments in silence, then nodded. "Have it your way. The lord knows you always do. I swear you've become more stubborn since William's death." She tilted her head to the side. "I suppose that was bound to happen, wasn't it? His actions, while shocking, affected us both in ways neither of us could have foreseen."

"That they did," Eden agreed. William had always been selfish, but that had been the worst thing he'd ever done, and it had led to his death. "At least he had the good sense to ensure we are both taken care of, and that Caden has a suitable guardian for his estates until he reaches his majority." Eden had funds of her own, so she didn't need to seek anything from her son's guardian, Roslyn had a dowry set up by her father, but William had added to it. It was almost as if he had known his scandalous behavior might prove a detriment to his younger sister.

"I'm done with the hem, Lady Roslyn," the seamstress said. "We can remove this gown and then start on the next one."

Roslyn nodded, and the seamstress helped her out of the gown. Eden sighed. This afternoon would never end... She would survive it, though. Roslyn depended on her, and she wouldn't be another selfish person in the young girl's life. Neither of them had a parent they could rely on. Roslyn was already in the next gown with the seamstress pinning where the alterations needed to be made when Eden snapped back to attention.

"Is Claudine going to visit again soon?" Roslyn asked.

Claudine Grant was another widow who had befriended Roslyn. She had come to visit while they prepared for Roslyn's debut season. She had left when her husband's father noticed her in Hyde Park. Since Claudine avoided her father-in-law, she had bolted. "I think she is to return soon." There would be a meeting with other widows that Claudine would need to attend at the Dowager Countess of

Wyndam's in the next week. "But I don't believe she'll be coming to Moreland House."

"Oh," Roslyn said, a little crestfallen. "I like her. We should at least invite her to dinner."

That was a splendid idea, but she didn't know if Claudine would want to stay in London long. She would likely wish to return to the widows' estate, Matron Manor, that the Widow's League owned. Eden had been invited to join the league after William's death, and it had been her saving grace. Amongst other widows, she'd discovered what she truly wanted for her life. Recently, she had even been bold enough to attend a masquerade filled with scandalous behavior. Her cheeks heated as she remembered that night. It was one she would never forget, and also never tell another soul about. It was her secret. One she relished more than she wanted to admit. "I can invite her, but I cannot guarantee she'll accept."

"All we can do is ask," Roslyn replied, then shrugged. "I do hope she accepts, but I understand if she cannot."

Eden smiled. Roslyn was very much unlike William. He was selfish and only thought about himself. His sister was kind and loving. How could two siblings be so dissimilar? She hoped that Caden wouldn't be anything like his father. It was her job as his mother to ensure that he would make better choices. Her son was her sole focus. "I'll send her a missive when we return home." Eden was almost certain she was already at Lady Wyndam's, but even if she wasn't, she would be soon.

Roslyn nodded and returned her attention to the seamstress. Eden found a nearby chair and plopped down on it, overheated and exhausted. After this fitting, they should be ready for the season. If only Eden was prepared for the vacuous gossip of some of the *ton's* leading matrons...

MAXWELL HOLDEN, THE DUKE OF CARRINGTON, STARED down at the missive on his desk. His mother was being her normal tedious self... She didn't come to town often, but apparently, she was going to deign to present her person in London, and soon. It was enough to drive a man to drink. Especially when his mother decided to meddle, and she most definitely intended to.

Apparently, she had decided it was time that Max found a wife. While he understood the reasoning, and happened to agree with her, he'd never admit as much to the woman. She would become even more unbearable then. He didn't want a wife, but he knew he wanted one. He had become guardian to his niece, Sarah, over a year ago. She'd been young enough that having a nanny to take care of her had been adequate, but now he realized she needed more than that. The little girl required a mother.

Which meant he would have to marry. He cursed his brother for dying. Sarah's mother, Caroline, had died giving birth to her. Caroline had never known her mother, and Max's brother, Owen, had barely paid any attention to his daughter. He'd drank himself into oblivion every day after his wife's death. If Max hadn't hired a nanny for Sarah, he doubted Owen ever would have. His brother had lived that way for several years before his behavior had caught up with him. He'd had one too many glasses or decanters of brandy and went riding in a storm. The horse had become spooked and thrown him. Owen's neck had broken on impact.

Sarah had become his responsibility the moment she'd been born, but he'd been able to pretend for a time it hadn't. He had hired the nanny and went about living his life. Now he had to find a bloody wife so his niece could have a mother. He ran his hand through his hair and blew out an exasperated breath. He didn't want a wife. But when had what he wanted ever truly mattered?

He had too much responsibility in his life, and it had started before he even reached his majority. His father died when Max was barely five and ten. He'd never attended school beyond Eton, and had taken his place as the new duke immediately. His family depended on him. That was his duty, and now finding an appropriate wife was another task expected of him.

Perhaps he should have a few drinks himself. He shook that thought away. Max rarely overindulged in spirits. He had learned that lesson when his father, then brother, had died from too much excess. *Hell.* What was he going to do? Max gave in and poured two fingers of brandy into a glass. One drink wouldn't hurt...

"What are you brooding over?" Emmett North, the Marquess of Crawford, said as he sauntered into the room. "Pour me a glass, would you?"

Max shook his head, but did as his friend asked. He handed Crawford a glass of brandy, then sat back behind his desk. He set his own brandy down and asked, "Why are you here?"

"I heard you attended the Duke of Sinbrough's

masquerade a little while back," the marquess said in a casual tone. Max just stared at him. There was never anything casual about his friend. He was asking for a reason, but he didn't know what it could be.

"That was six weeks ago," he said. He kept his tone as neutral as Crawford's had been. He didn't want to let anything slip. "I've attended before."

"Not very often," Crawford replied, then sipped his brandy. "What made this one different?"

Damn... His friend was right. He hadn't gone to one of the Duke of Sinbrough's debauched events in quite a while. For the most part, it wasn't his type of ball. Honestly, no ball was one he liked to attend, but it had been important to him to go that night. It was when he first realized he would have to marry soon. It was like his last night of decadence before becoming the man who would soon have a woman he called his. He would never tell Crawford all of that. His friend would make it out to be something bigger than it actually was. He shrugged. "It seemed like a good idea at the time."

"And you don't think you should have gone now?" He lifted a brow. Crawford was mocking him, and he didn't know why.

"What are you really asking me?" Max didn't

have the patience for games. There was too much for him to decide, and the marquess wouldn't let this go easily.

"I heard you found yourself a woman." Crawford sat up straighter. "A blonde goddess that Sinbrough wanted for himself."

Max grinned at that. He had spent the evening with a blonde and it had been memorable. So much so that he'd thought of her every day since. It was too bad he didn't know her identity. He wouldn't mind a few more nights with her before he found himself a suitable wife. "The Duke of Sin unquestionably wanted her for himself." Max shrugged. "She hadn't been interested. The lady definitely had more refined taste."

Crawford barked in laughter. "Sinbrough does spread his love around more freely." He lifted a brow. "Who was she?"

He frowned. She hadn't told him her name, but he knew almost every inch of her body. Her mask had covered nearly her entire face. "I don't know."

"How is that possible?" Crawford downed his brandy, then grabbed the decanter to refill it. "You did spend the entire evening with her, did you not?"

He had... "I fell asleep, and she left before I awakened." Max really should have insisted she tell him her name. He'd been more inclined to ravish her at the time, though. "She never removed her mask. It's not like I attend those masquerades very often. I doubt I would know most of the people there." Or at least recognize them... "Some ladies prefer that their identities remain unknown."

"That is true," he agreed. "However, most of them at least tell their lovers their given name. This one didn't share at all?"

"No." He didn't need the reminder that he'd blundered. Max had given her pleasure, but he'd lost his mind when he'd seduced her. All he had been focused on was her and her delectable body. She'd been so bloody perfect. "If I could change that, I would. Why do you ask?" He hoped Crawford didn't want to bed the woman himself. He might have to beat his friend senseless if he did. Max thought of her as his, and yes, he knew he shouldn't. She didn't belong to him, but his desire for her was not yet quenched.

"It's probably nothing," he said. "I heard a rumor you were looking for a wife, and then, in the same discussion, the gentlemen were discussing your night at the masquerade. Some are wondering if you intend to marry her."

Max laughed. The gossip that went around the

ton could be ridiculous. "I do intend to marry," he told his friend. "It is time. Sarah needs a mother."

"But since you don't know Lady Seductress's name, you can't very well marry her." Crawford grinned. "I don't envy you searching for a suitable wife. Do you have anyone in mind?"

He shook his head. "None." He sipped his brandy. It burned as it traveled down his throat. "I have requirements, though."

"As you should." Crawford grinned. "Care to share them?"

"She has to be beautiful," he said. "If I have to marry, I want to like actually looking at the woman."

"That goes unsaid," the marquess agreed. "And the rest?"

"She should be biddable. I don't need a woman harping on me daily." That sounded like a damned nightmare. "I don't need an heiress, but I suppose it wouldn't hurt that she didn't need to marry me for my fortune." What else? "She also has to be kind and capable of loving a child that isn't hers. I won't have her neglecting Sarah when that is the very reason I am even considering marriage."

"So, to summarize," Crawford began. "You do not want a simpering young miss or an acerbic bluestocking, but something in-between. One with beauty and a flush dowry."

He glared at his friend. "You make it sound as if my list isn't attainable."

Crawford rolled his eyes. "Because none of those young debutantes are going to show you who they really are. All they will see is your title, and they'll pretend to be the type of woman you want. The only things on that list of yours you will be able to check off immediately are the beauty and the dowry. You're going to need help with the rest."

Bloody hell... "Are you volunteering?"

Crawford wrinkled his nose. "I'll speak with Lyonsdale. Between the two of us, we can uncover the rest. Just let us know which young ladies catch your attention, and we will investigate them for you."

"Thank you," he told his friend. The Earl of Lyonsdale, Crawford, and him had been inseparable since they met at Eton. "I appreciate your assistance in this." Max's wife would have to be the most suitable woman he could find. His young niece had enough upheaval in her young life. He lifted his glass. "To finding me a wife."

Crawford held up his glass. "To surviving the season."

They both drank the rest of their brandy, then set down their glasses. It would be an interesting season. Crawford had that last bit correct. There wasn't much that slid past the marquess. He had an uncanny ability to see through everyone and everything.

Acknowledgments

Special thanks to Elizabeth Evans. Your encouragement and assistance with this book helped me immensely. I am grateful for all you do for me.

About Dawn Brower

USA TODAY Bestselling author, DAWN BROWER writes both historical and contemporary romance. There are always stories inside her head; she just never thought she could make them come to life. That creativity has finally found an outlet.

Growing up, she was the only girl out of six children. She raised two boys as a single mother; there is never a dull moment in her life. Reading books is her favorite hobby, and she loves all genres.

www.authordawnbrower.com
TikTok: @1DawnBrower

- bookbub.com/authors/dawn-brower
- facebook.com/1DawnBrower
- x.com/1DawnBrower
- instagram.com/1DawnBrower
- goodreads.com/dawnbrower

Also by Dawn Brower

HISTORICAL

Stand alone:

Broken Pearl

A Wallflower's Christmas Kiss

A Gypsy's Christmas Kiss

Marsden Romances

A Flawed Jewel

A Crystal Angel

A Treasured Lily

A Sanguine Gem

A Hidden Ruby

A Discarded Pearl

Marsden Descendants

Rebellious Angel

Tempting An American Princess

How to Kiss a Debutante

Loving an America Spy

Linked Across Time

Saved by My Blackguard

Searching for My Rogue

Seduction of My Rake

Surrendering to My Spy

Spellbound by My Charmer

Stolen by My Knave

Separated from My Love

Scheming with My Duke

Secluded with My Hellion

Secrets of My Beloved

Spying on My Scoundrel

Shocked by My Vixen

Smitten with My Christmas Minx

Vision of Love

Enduring Legacy

The Legacy's Origin

Charming Her Rogue

Ever Beloved

Forever My Earl

Always My Viscount

Infinitely My Marquess

Eternally My Duke

Bluestockings Defying Rogues

When An Earl Turns Wicked

A Lady Hoyden's Secret

One Wicked Kiss

Earl In Trouble

All the Ladies Love Coventry

One Less Scandalous Earl

Confessions of a Hellion

The Vixen in Red

Lady Pear's Duke

Scandal Meets Love

Love Only Me (Amanda Mariel)

Find Me Love (Dawn Brower)

If It's Love (Amanda Mariel)

Odds of Love (Dawn Brower)

Believe In Love (Amanda Mariel)

Chance of Love (Dawn Brower)

Love and Holly (Amanda Mariel)

Love and Mistletoe (Dawn Brower

The Neverhartts

Never Defy a Vixen

Never Disregard a Wallflower

Never Dare a Hellion

Never Deceive a Bluestocking

Never Disrespect a Governess

Never Desire a Duke

CONTEMPORARY

Stand alone:

Deadly Benevolence

Snowflake Kisses

Kindred Lies

Sparkle City

Diamonds Don't Cry

Hooking a Firefly

Novak Springs

Cowgirl Fever

Dirty Proof

Unbridled Pursuit

Sensual Games

Christmas Temptation

Daring Love

Passion and Lies

Desire and Jealousy

Seduction and Betrayal

Begin Again

There You'll Be

Better as a Memory

Won't Let Go

Heart's Intent

One Heart to Give

Unveiled Hearts

Heart of the Moment

Kiss My Heart Goodbye

Heart in Waiting

Heart Lessons

A Heart Redeemed

Kismet Bay

Once Upon a Christmas

New Year Revelation

All Things Valentine

Luck At First Sight

Endless Summer Days

A Witch's Charm

All Out of Gratitude

Christmas Ever After

YOUNG ADULT FANTASY

Broken Curses

The Enchanted Princess

The Bespelled Knight

The Magical Hunt